TEXAS SHOWDOWN

A WESTERN ADVENTURE

TIMBER: U.S. MARSHAL

ROBERT HANLON   CHARLES RAY

J.W. MASTERSON

1

OTHO WATKINS WHISTLED the tune "Buffalo Gals" as he sat at the throttle of The East Texas Flyer, the fastest passenger train riding the tracks from Fort Worth Texas to Nacogdoches, Texas. No other train on those tracks came close to The Flyer's speed. After twenty years of engineering trains all over Texas, Otho was justifiably proud to be the main engineer on The Flyer. Watching the countryside fly by on this gorgeous spring day, Otho was a happy contented man. Pulling his watch out of the pocket in his overalls and looking at it he said, "Burl, you can ease off a bit and take a break. We're so far ahead of schedule, we can afford to slack off some. It wouldn't look good to be too early getting to Nacogdoches. The big bosses would start expectin' us to arrive early every time."

The big black fireman standing next to him dug a long red rag out of his back pocket and wiped his face and sweat-covered upper body. Returning the damp rag to his pocket he flexed his massive shoulders and stretched his arms. "

Summer be just around the corner, Otho," he said in a voice that sounded like it came from the bottom of a well. "I sure ain't lookin' forward to it. It already gets hot 'nuff in this iron cave to make the devil sweat. Summer times ain't no fun."

"I agree with you there Burl but look at it this way. When you get home and take that cold rainwater shower then your sweet Mandy rubs that big ol' back of yours I'd say it don't get no better than that." Burl laughed. "Yes sir, that's what makes this job worth doin'." He lifted a dipperful of tepid water out of their water barrel, drank some then poured the rest over his head.

"Now that Miss Bessie's gone, what you do when you ain't workin' Otho?"

"I play with my dogs some and I read a whole lot. I've always enjoyed readin' the likes of Jules Verne, Alexandre Dumas, James Fenimore Coo..."

The big fireman interrupted Otho. "We got riders comin' fast on the right side Boss. They's wavin' guns in the air."

"Dang it!" said the engineer. "We got more comin' in from the left. Been a long while since we were robbed. I reckon we're about due." He blew the whistle three times in a row to alert the conductor and the rest of the crew to the eminent attack then began to slow the great coal eating beast down.

"Ain't no use tryin' to outrun em, Burl. We'll stop and let them go about their business then be on our way."

Burl spat out the side of the cab. "I can't hardly stand by and do nothin' while them owl hoots rob our passengers. It goes agin' my upbrigin'."

"I don't like it either," said the engineer frowning, "but I'd like to go on livin'."

As the East Texas Flyer rolled to a stop, men rode up on each side of the cab. A man on the right side dismounted and handed the reins of his chestnut gelding to another rider. He climbed into the cab.

"Afternoon fellers," he said. "Y'all stay still and keep your hands where I can see 'em." He thumbed back the hammer of his .44. "Everything goes okay y'all be back on the road in no time." He eyed Burl standing with a grim look on his face. "You sure are a big 'un ain't you feller? I bet you'd like to get them giant callused paws around my neck wouldn't you. Forget it, it ain't gonna happen."

The train carried three half-filled passenger cars and a caboose.

Two men robbed the workers in the caboose of any valuables they might have while three more started in the back passenger car and worked their way forward. Two of the men relieved the passengers of their money, watches, and jewelry. The third man held a gun in each hand and pointed them at the passengers.

"Chance, you and Willie make sure to collect any weapons you find. I don't want it to happen like last time when that stupid pilgrim tried to plug me and I had to kill him. Everybody stay calm," he said to the passengers. "All the money in the world ain't worth your life."

The man in the cab hollered to his companion outside. "Any sign of 'em finishing yet, Buster?"

The mounted robber shook his head. "Not yet but you need to hurry up, Wade. This is takin' way too long."

"Hold your horses, boy. We'll be finished when Butch says we're finished." He turned his attention back to the captives in the cab. "It's about time I see what you two got to donate to our charity." A wicked laugh emerged from his mouth.

"All I have is this old watch," said Otho. "You are welcome to it. It don't keep good time anyhow. You're welcome to search me but you won't find nothin' but a boloney sandwich.

The outlaw reached out and took the watch. "Give me that sandwich too. I ain't eaten in a coon's age." He took the sandwich, threw the wrapper on the floor and took a big bite. Looking at Burl he swallowed the first bite and took another. "

Sorry about that coon remark. We got one of your people ridin' with us. He don't like it when I say 'coon' neither, but Erastus he don't say nothin' 'cause he knows I'd send him to that great cotton patch in the sky in a Texas minute." He laughed again and finished off the bologna sandwich.

"Somethin' you and Erastus got in common with all the other dark folks is the bunch of y'all ain't good for nothing but doin' what people tell you to."

Burl jumped at the man. Anticipating the fireman's move the outlaw fired three bullets into the big black man's chest before he took two steps. The fireman stared down at his chest then dropped to his knees and fell on his face.

"Big ol' rascals like this 'un," said the outlaw, "you always got to be careful they ain't still alive." He fired a round into the back of Burl's head. "That ought to do it."

"You son-of-a-bitch," said Otho. "That man has a wife and two children. If I was younger, I'd go for you too."

The outlaw pointed his .44 at Otho. "And you'd be dead as your fireman. Now, shut your mouth and don't say nothin' else."

"Wade, Ollie's wavin'," said the man holding the killer's horse. "Let's get the hell out of here."

"Good to meet you, Mr. Engineer," said Wade. "Maybe, I'll see you again sometime soon. We work on a regular basis." He started down the steps but stopped on the bottom one. "You tell the stupid darky's wife that if he hadn't been so sensitive about the color of his skin, he would still be alive." Climbing aboard his big chestnut he waved, and the outlaws took off at a gallop.

The two men in the caboose rode off at the same time. The three who robbed the passenger cars stood on the platform between the last car and the caboose. Two of the men mounted their horses and followed the rest up into the hills. The one called Ollie had trouble holding his horse and the reins to the other one. Both animals wanted to follow the rest.

"Come on, Butch," he yelled. "We needs to go." His fat gut bounced on the saddle horn and he winced every time.

Ollie was the older brother of the man in the car, Butch Farnum who was the leader of the gang. Ollie had been dropped on his head as an infant and it affected his intelligence in a negative way. Whatever Butch said Ollie did without question. One of his biggest problems was he couldn't stand pressure of any kind. He was almost ready to panic.

"I'm comin' Fat. Hold on." Butch Farnum bowed to the people in the car. "Ladies and gentlemen, you have just had the privilege of bein' relieved of your valuables by the famous Farnum gang of which

I am the leader, Butch Farnum. Please tell your children and grand-children about the experience. Until we meet again, *Adios*."

Just as Butch Farnum leaned out and reached for his reins, his fat brother had a panic attack, he let go of Butch's horse which took off. Losing his balance, the outlaw leader tumbled from the platform and landed on his head. Knocked cold by the fall, Butch Farnum lay face down in the dirt. A nervous passenger stepped between the cars and looked down at the unconscious man.

"Not so tough looking now are you Farnum," he said and spit at the outlaw leader. "I reckon you'll hang for this. He scratched the stubble on his jaw. "Hmmm, I wonder if there is a reward?"

Even though he was a Texan, Butch Farnum believed in keeping the United States intact, so when the Civil War began he chose to head north and join the Union Army. Farnum was a smart, resourceful man. Because of his bravery in multiple battles he rapidly rose through the ranks so by the end of the conflict he had attained the rank of Colonel. Living through the nightmare of battle and experiencing the carnage and devastation of war, Farnum changed from a man who respected law and order to a ruthless criminal who took anything he wanted no matter what the cost in destruction of property or loss of human life. Over time he assembled a gang of killers and bandits gaining a reputation as the most notorious gang in East Texas. The merciless outlaw leader led his gang on dozens of bank, train, and stagecoach robberies. They seemed unstoppable but due to a quirk of fate during their most recent robbery the gang leader was captured and taken to Nacogdoches where he awaited transfer to Austin to stand trial for robbery and murder.

XXXXX

Texas Ranger Captain, Benjamin Tolliver eyed the young man sitting across from his desk. Tall and angular with an unruly shock of blond hair jutting out from under his hat. Joe Don Horton had proven himself to be a good Ranger in the year he had been a member of the elite organization. Captain Tolliver had picked the young Ranger to take on the dangerous task of bringing the outlaw Butch Farnum to Austin from Nacogdoches aboard the train to face trial.

"Ranger Horton, I don't hand out assignments without giving them a lot of thought," said the captain. "I picked you for this task because I know you are capable of taking care of the situation." As was his habit when handing out assignments Captain Tolliver removed a long black, Cuban cigar from his desk drawer bit off one end, and stuck the cigar in his mouth. After lighting it he puffed a few times to get it going good then blew a series of blue smoke rings into the stale office air.

"You will take the five o'clock train to Nacogdoches this afternoon. When you get there go straight to the sheriff's office. Sheriff Stevens will be waiting for you. He will go with you and the prisoner to the train station and make sure y'all catch the next train to Austin. When you reach Austin two Rangers will be waiting at the station to help you take Farnum to jail. Right now only Sheriff Stevens, you, and myself know about this arrangement."

Captain Tolliver enjoyed his cigars and he liked to think the use of them while he handed out assignments enhanced his position as *the* man in charge. He felt like the long, black Cuban cigars enhanced his professionalism. "Any questions Ranger Horton?"

"No sir," said Horton with an austere look on his face. He stood up. "I appreciate your confidence in me Captain Tolliver. I won't let you down."

The captain stood and shook the young man's hand. "I'm sure you will do fine. See you in two days. Safe travel."

XXXXX

RANGER HORTON BOARDED the train fifteen minutes early. Finding his seat he sat back and mentally prepared himself for the task at hand. A long, twelve-hour train ride lay ahead of him. After an hour or two in Nacogdoches he would have to endure another twelve-hour ride back to Austin, this time with a prisoner. Getting as much sleep as possible on the way there was a priority.

After a year I have a mission where I'm in charge. It's just me but still I don't have to take orders from anyone. Except for the lousy hours this mission ought to go down without a hitch. The young Ranger stretched. *Reckon I'd better start tryin' to get some shuteye. I'll sleep a couple hours then I'll eat that supper Susie fixed for me. She sure is a good cook. She doesn't know it but when I get back to Austin I'm gonna ask her to marry me. Maybe her daddy, Preacher Stolworthy will marry us in his church. I think Susie will like that just fine.*

After getting off the train in Nacogdoches Ranger Horton got directions to the sheriff's office. Stepping inside he addressed a man sitting behind a desk at the back of the office. "Sheriff Stevens?"

The large, rotund man rubbed his eyes as if he had been sleeping. "I'm Stevens. What can I do for you young man?"

Joe Don strode forward and laid his credentials on the desk. "I'm Ranger Joe Don Horton from Austin here to pick up Butch Farnum."

Sheriff Stevens handed the credentials back to Joe Don. "Everything looks in order Ranger Horton. Farnum's in the back. Your captain wired me when to expect you so I got two tickets on the seven a.m. train." He pulled out his pocket watch. "Looks like she leaves in little over an hour. We'll go to the station at the last minute. I don't think anyone has a clue about what we're doing but it can't hurt to take every precaution." With difficulty the sheriff raised his enormous bulk out of the chair. He stood for a moment like he was working on getting his balance. "It's been a long night and I need some more coffee. You want a cup, Ranger?" Joe Don nodded.

"How 'bout a cup for the condemned prisoner, sheriff?" came a deep, resonant voice from the cell block. "Outlaws drink coffee, too."

"I ain't gettin' you one doggone thing more Farnum. Only reason I been feedin' you is because the law says I have to but it don't say a thing about coffee." Sheriff Stevens spat on the floor. "After what y'all did to poor Burl Tedrow I'd just as soon see you starve to death."

"I done told you 'Porky', that wasn't me. I was in the back of the train when that happened. Only reason I know about it is 'cause you told me. I may rob folks for a livin' but I ain't no murderer."

The sheriff got their coffee and waddled back to his desk where he eased into his chair. He and Joe Don drank their coffee in silence. When it was time to go the two men got up and walked back to the cell holding Butch Farnum. Joe Don held his gun pointed at the prisoner while the sheriff opened the cell, stepped inside and handcuffed Farnum's hands behind his back. During the whole time the outlaw stayed silent.

Opening the office front door, Sheriff Stevens peered outside. The town had just begun to awaken and few people occupied the street. "Come on Ranger," said the sheriff. "We got to get y'all to the train as fast as we can."

The three men hit the street at a fast walk and in ten minutes Joe Don and his prisoner were sitting in their seats across from each other in the last passenger car on the train. As the train started off the steam engine smoking like the world's biggest chimney. Joe Don looked out the window. He watched the train pass the sheriff who stood watching with a peculiar look on his face. "Wonder what he's thinking?" He said to himself.

"What'd you say, Ranger?" asked Farnum.

"Nothin' important. We got a long ride ahead of us Farnum. I suggest you get as much sleep as you can. Makes the trip go by quicker."

"Yes sir Mr. Ranger." The outlaw smiled. "Whatever you say Mr. Ranger. I figure we'll get to know each other a whole lot better before this trip is done but right now, I'll do whatever you say Mr. Ranger."

2

JOE DON HORTON JOLTED AWAKE. Try as hard as he could to keep his eyes open the young Ranger dozed off now and then. This time when he awoke he felt something was different but he couldn't figure out what it was. Daylight streamed through the coach window as it had been for some time now. He looked over at Butch Farnum who seemed to be snoring peacefully. The young Ranger noticed the conductor coming down the aisle swaying while he walked, keeping his balance with the constant movement of the train.

"Pardon me, Sir," said Joe Don, as the little man reached the area where he was sitting. "Would you happen to have the time?"

The conductor smiled, revealing a perfect set of teeth. "Of course," he said, never losing his smile. "It is precisely two fourteen in the afternoon on this glorious East Texas spring day and I must say we are running on time as usual. Our railroad takes pride in our trains always being on time." The conductor took off his hat, revealing a shiny bald head with a little fringe of gray hair around the sides. He scratched the top of his head and returned the hat adjusting it until he felt it looked just right. "I have been a conductor on this company's trains for thirty-five years and I can count on the fingers of one hand the times we have been late. That's a record that is hard to beat." He started to walk away but stopped in mid stride. "That's odd. We seem to be slowing down. We are forty-five minutes from our next scheduled stop. I must go see Mr. Paulsen, our engineer and see if something is amiss." The little man scurried toward the front of the train.

Joe Don watched the conductor walk away. *I wonder why we're slowing down. Probably some cattle crossing the track or something like that, but just in case, I'd better have my .45 out and ready.*

Just before the conductor reached the front of the car a man stepped inside the back of the car and fired two shots into the conductor's back. The little man groaned and pitched forward onto his face. Joe Don jerked his .45 up and fired at the killer. He shot too fast and the bullet ricocheted off the wall. The man ducked out of the doorway.

Women passengers were screaming and men were ducking behind the seats. Joe Don dropped to the floor and kept his eye on the car's back door. Without looking he said, "Farnum, if you even twitch you're a dead man."

"I ain't in this," said the outlaw with his head down and hugging the floor.

There were no more gunshots for a moment. Joe Don raised his head a little bit to peek at the back of the car. A gun fired and a neat round hole popped open in the back of the Ranger's head. Joe Don slumped to the floor.

"Come on in fellers, I got him." The speaker, Wade Morgan was the man who killed the fireman the day Butch Farnum got captured. Two outlaws edged in the back door. Another came in behind Morgan who had entered the front of the car and snuck up behind Joe Don.

"'Bout time y'all got here Chance," said Butch.

A year younger than Butch, Chance Farnum, the good-looking one of the four brothers fancied himself as quite the ladies' man. Ollie and Willie Bob were the others. Ollie, the oldest, having been dropped on his head couldn't think very well. His brothers were mean to him and called him "half-wit". What Butch said Ollie took as gospel. Willie Bob the youngest, was a loose cannon with a 'little man' syndrome. Fast with a gun and much smaller than his three brothers Willie Bob was given the nickname, "Little Willie". The moniker stuck and the young man despised it.

"Willie Bob," said Chance, "get over yonder and search through the dead Ranger's pockets and find the key to unlock the handcuffs. The young man found them in the first pocket he looked through and unlocked the cuffs.

Butch stood up stretched, and rubbed his wrists where the handcuffs had chaffed them. "Took you mutton heads long enough. It ain't a lot of fun wearin' handcuffs. My gun belt and gun are back in Nacogdoches. Willie Bob take off the Ranger's rig and hand it to me."

The youngest Farnum brother removed the holster from Joe Don's body and picked his revolver up off the floor.

"Here you are, Butch. It sure is good to see you alive. After your horse showed up in camp riderless we didn't know what to think. We knew Ollie was holdin' him waitin' for you to get off the train. Chance asked him if you made it off all right and that half-wit said he didn't know. Said when he took off he was too scared to look back."

Butch rubbed a big hand down his scruffy face. "That fat piece of shit turned loose of my horse just as I was reachin' for him. I fell, and next thing I knew I was in that stinkin' jail cell in Nacogdoches." The gang leader looked around. "Where is he?"

"We left him at the camp," said Chance. "I didn't want him screwin' up here like he did the other day."

"That's right thinkin' little brother. It's good to know somebody else in this family has got a brain." Butch strapped on Joe Don's rig. He pulled the gun out and checked it over. "This here iron is a Colt .45. Looks nearly brand new." He spun the cylinder. "I believe I'm gonna like it just fine."

"It's a cinch the previous owner won't mind," said Wade Morgan, an evil smile crossing his features. The members of the gang laughed.

"All right, boys," said Butch, "we're wastin' time. Let's rob the passengers and get the hell out of here. I need a cup of coffee."

3

U.S. MARSHAL JAKE TIMBER had just finished being assigned to the army for a job over at Fort Croghan and he was now kicking his heels for a spell in South Fork taking a well-earned rest and a few beers. He knew he had to send a telegram to his boss over in Austin. His boss was the governor of Texas; the Honorable Robert Pierce Fullerton. He knew the governor was expecting him to send a telegram so draining his glass he left the saloon he was in, mounted up on his big bay gelding, Scout and headed down the street to the Telegraph Office.

Walking inside he saw the operator was hammering out a message for another man. A youth was sitting at a desk just inside the door who looked up at the big man wearing deerskins and incongruously black boots with tin toe and heel caps. He also noticed the double rig of Colts strapped around his waist.

"Can I help ya sir?" He asked.

"I'm here to send a telegram," Timber said bluntly and unnecessarily.

"Okay sir. If you'd like to give it to me I'll get Mister Clarke on it right away," he said picking up a pad and pen.

Timber told the young man what he wanted to send. The telegram was one he had promised to wire to the governor who had assigned him to the fort in order to assist in the capture of an outlaw Timber knew and had arrested two years ago only to have him broken out of prison by his outlaw gang. The governor had wanted to know the outcome of straightening out the gang who had been causing mayhem in northern Texas from Timber's point of view although he would get a report from the fort commander. Now Timber could get that done.

It wasn't until Timber told the boy who the telegram was from that he heard he was a marshal as Timber wasn't wearing his badge. He figured it best if most of the time he kept it in a shirt pocket, no use in giving any young gunman trying to make a name for himself or an outlaw a target to shoot at.

It wasn't unusual for Timber to report in to the governor as it was usually the only means of contact between them. Often Fullerton would send telegrams for Timber to places where he was known to be with information or things he wanted him to do. Now that Timber had wired him he would wait somewhere in case there was any reply as that often happened.

"If you get a reply to that would you bring it to me? I'll be at Rawlings Saloon." Timber told the youth.

"Sure thing marshal," he replied, "just as soon as it comes in."

Timber thanked him, paid for the telegram and walked back out into the hot sun. He rode down to the saloon to wait and see if a reply came from the governor. It was still early in the day although Timber had eaten breakfast at a restaurant having spent the last night in the hotel. Soft beds were always a luxury when he could get one. So neither being hungry or thirsty he considered sitting outside the saloon to wait on the Telegraph boy but then changed his mind and went inside. He went over to the bar where the bartender was waiting to serve him.

"What'll it be?" The man asked.

"Coffee will be just fine," Timber said.

The bartender gave him a long look, "Mister we sell beer, whiskey and wines among a few other things but we don't sell coffee."

Timber returned the look and leaned in closer to him, "I asked for coffee and that's what I want."

The bartender held his gaze as long as he could then looked away, "Okay already, coffee it is," he strode off along the bar grumbling to himself. He got the coffee from a room in the back and brought it out to Timber.

"There you go, one coffee. That'll be two bits."

Timber dropped the coins on the bar and took his cup to a table that gave him a view of most of the saloon and more importantly, the door. There weren't many men in the saloon due to the time of day which suited him just fine. He sat down and pulled a battered pack of playing cards from a pocket and laid them out for a game of solitaire. Then he settled down to play and wait.

It was a good hour and a half before a reply came which in the circumstances was still pretty quick. Timber was into his third cup before it happened. He looked up as the boy entered the saloon and walked over to him.

"Marshal Timber I have a reply for you," he said holding it out for him.

Timber took it as the boy waited expectantly in case Timber wanted to reply to it.

Opening it up he stared at the piece of paper:

To U.S. Marshal Jake Timber:

There is a particularly savage gang of outlaws terrorizing the area around Palestine. I want them stopped and I want you there to do it. To help you out I have arranged for a deputy marshal by the name of Bass Reeves to meet you there. According to my information the gang is led by a Butch Farnum. From where you are you should be able to meet Reeves there later today, tomorrow morning latest. Reeves will meet you at the Grand Hotel. Keep me informed.

The Honorable Robert Pierce Fullerton

Texas Governor

Timber read it twice then folded it up and put it in a pocket. Then he looked at the boy.

"No reply," he said.

The boy turned to go when Timber called him back and gave him a dollar piece.

"For your trouble."

"Gee thanks marshal," the boy smiled at him and hurried on out.

Timber was happy enough to go to Palestine and look for the outlaws but he wasn't so pleased about being teamed up with another marshal, a deputy one at that. Timber liked to work alone. He didn't make friends easy in fact he didn't make friends. The only friend he had was his horse, Scout. However he was willing to do what the governor asked him to as he always did. He had been sent on assignments before where he'd had to meet up with others, the army being the latest one. He was never happy working with someone else as he felt he couldn't trust another man and they only got in the way. However he knew he would catch a train for the six hour ride up to Palestine and see what he could do. He just hoped this deputy marshal he was meeting would be worthy of the task they had to do.

Having heard from the governor it brought to mind what had brought him to where he was. It all started from the night his wife and daughter were killed, in revenge for Timber stopping a maniac from killing a barmaid. Since that night Timber struggled to sleep more than an hour or two at a time. Many nights he'd pass on sleeping completely. He would take his horse, go for a long ride, and return just as the sun was rising. He was no longer plagued by the recurrent nightmares he'd suffered for years after the death of his first wife and child, but he still had them now and then.

He had been a prisoner at the Great Falls Penitentiary for the murder of Cain Gentry who had killed his wife and daughter. Timber had killed him the next day by burning the house down he was in after breaking his back and beating him to a pulp; he had prevented the man's rescue by his deputies as at the time Timber had been a sheriff. Then, the Texas governor, a personal friend of Gentry's, was caught stealing from the treasury, and a new governor came into power. He pardoned Timber, on the condition that he use his unique

talents with a gun to hunt down the criminals and wanted men in
Texas to have crime under control a lot more.

When Timber had been in prison he had spent the nights sitting
in the dark, reliving the hellish nightmare his life had become while
weeping silently in his cell. His life regained its purpose when the
governor, Robert Fullerton charged the Honorable Milton Westbrook
the chief justice of the court to make Timber a special agent of the
court to clean up the backlog of wanted men in Texas and set aside
his personal vendetta. It had been the most difficult decision he had
ever made. In the end, he figured it would be better to fight the good
fight in the daylight rather than fight an unreachable, unbeatable foe
in the dark each night. Upon his release, the judge handed him a
piece of paper, and Timber was sworn in as a special agent of the
court. To be controlled by the Texas governor. Then he was turned
loose to wander around wherever he wanted, eliminating those who
were predators and criminals. He wasn't charged with bringing them
to court for trial; he was charged with dispersing justice from the
barrel of a gun. If a man was wanted by the law or should have been,
Jake Timber was authorized to administer justice with all the
lethality he could muster. He was a bounty hunter with a territorial
mandate, which gave him extreme latitude in dealing with criminals
and wanted men. He had been charged with the elimination of
wanted men. There will be no court hearings for the men he finds—
he was basically charged with killing them in any manner he deemed
efficient. He carried a U.S Marshal badge in a pocket along with his
papers of authority signed by the Texas Governor, the Honorable
Robert Pierce Fullerton. He was an independent law enforcement
officer, who was above the law and reported directly to the governor.
He had the power to arrest, detain, or execute criminal individuals as
he saw fit. This included any local law enforcement, or locally elected
or appointed official who attempted, in any way, to interfere with his
official duties.

Timber finished his coffee and walked out of the saloon. It was
getting on for midday so he figured there was time to get to Palestine
provided the train times matched up. He mounted Scout and rode

out of town heading for the railroad and a station in which to board it.

He came to a terminal just outside of town and went to the ticket office only to be told that he was unlucky in that the train had already pulled out so he bought a ticket for the ride north for the next day which would be leaving at noon. He then rode back into town to rest up, grab a few beers, play solitaire and spend some time with Scout.

The next morning he paid his dues at the hotel, had breakfast, collected Scout from the livery and then rode out to the railroad terminal. He got there as the train was due to pull out in just half an hour's time. He got Scout safely into a stock car for the journey before he found a seat in a passenger car. He found a seat where he could sit alone to watch the view through the window. Then he settled down for the ride.

After a few miles the conductor came along to check his ticket. He looked hard at Timber but didn't say anything and was about to carry on when Timber called him back.

"You from Palestine?" He asked.

"Yeah, when I get to be there," the conductor answered.

"If there's more 'n one hotel which one is the best?"

"There's a few hotels in Palestine, you never been there afore?"

"No, that's why I'm askin'."

"Well then the Grand Hotel is for you," he said that looking at Timber's deerskins wondering if he would be allowed in the place.

"Okay that's good enough," Timber answered as he lowered his hat to catch an hour's sleep to the rumble and clickety clack of the train.

The conductor mumbled to himself and walked on.

It seemed a long time to Timber before the train finally came to a halt in Palestine belching out smoke and steam as it came to a rest. Timber alighted quickly and made his way down to the stock car where he got Scout out. Then it was away out of the station in search of the Grand Hotel hoping it would be as good as the name said it should.

Palestine turned out to be a hell of a place with lots of streets and fine buildings. It was busy too and Timber had to ask more than once to find the hotel. He finally pulled up outside and leaving Scout at the rail he went in. It was decorated in fine wallpaper; the drapes were thick velvet and there was a carpet on the floor. Timber walked over to the desk where the clerk was waiting for him.

"Has a Bass Reeves checked in?" He asked.

"I'm sorry sir but I'm not at liberty to give out that information, unless you are kin?" The clerk looked back at him taking in his clothes, shirt and trousers of buckskin and the wide brown hat on his head.

Timber pulled his marshal badge from a pocket and flashed it at the clerk.

"Marshal Jake Timber. I'm waiting on a deputy marshal Bass Reeves, now has he checked in yet?"

The clerk suddenly pulled the register towards him to take a look, "No sir, I'm sorry he hasn't."

"I'll need a room and I'll wait for him." Timber stood waiting for the clerk to answer.

"Certainly marshal," he gave Timber a pen to sign in with. He wasn't sure he should let him in as he was dressed in buckskins but then he was a lawman. He snagged a key from the pigeon holes behind him and held it out, "There we are marshal. How many nights are you staying?"

"Can't tell right now. I'll let you know," Timber took the offered key and went off for the stairs to check the room out leaving the clerk staring after him.

4

"YA SURE YA DON' wanna take the stage to Longview 'n then get a train down to Palestine, deputy," the bewhiskered clerk said as he peered over the top of his rimless spectacles at Deputy U.S. Marshal Bass Reeves.

Bass mulled over the suggestion. The ride south to Palestine from Paris Texas, was four days and the train ride could take two but he'd be cramped in a passenger car with who knows how many other people for those two days. He'd come from Fort Smith, Arkansas to Paris by horse, a five-day ride and it had been enjoyable. He shrugged

"No, I'm fine with ridin'," he said. "I'll need to draw travel money for eight days. Four down 'n four back. Plus expenses for maybe a week.

That was his best estimate for the job he was being sent to do, a job whose specific outlines were still blurred

"Suit yerself," said the clerk. "Ya ain't gonna find a lotta places twixt here 'n Palestine that ya kin rent a room though.

Bass knew that. There were precious few places in Paris, site of the U.S. Court for Eastern Texas, where a black man was welcome to spend the night. The black community of the town, though signifi-cant, was economically deprived and few had spare room to house a stranger. The U.S. Marshal for the district, Harvey Mudd, had set up sleeping places in the marshal's stable to accommodate Bass and some of the other black deputies who'd been recently hired by Judge Isaac Parker of the U.S. Court for Western Arkansas and Indian Territory in Fort Smith. It didn't bother him, though. He much preferred sleeping under the stars when he couldn't sleep in his own bed anyway

As a former enslaved man who'd escaped to Indian Territory shortly after the Civil War started he'd long since learned to survive in the wild. It was like a second home to him

What he had issues with though was the uncertainty and fuzziness in the instructions he'd received from Mudd.

XXXXX

"Have a seat Bass," Mudd told him.

Bass gently lowered his six-foot-two, two-hundred pounds frame into the wooden chair next to Mudd's desk and balanced his gray wide-brimmed hat on his knee

"You wanted to see me marshal?" he asked curious as to why he'd been summoned to the marshal's office.

He'd been sent to Paris from Fort Smith to give testimony in the trial of two rustlers he'd helped deputies from Paris capture in the Cherokee Nation in Indian Territory. He'd just finished testifying and was heading to the space in the livery stable where he'd been bunking to pack so he could get an early start the next day for home, so as far as he knew there was no other business he had in Paris

"I received a telegram from the governor's office," Mudd said. "There's apparently some gang operating here in East Texas that the governor's worried about enough to send a marshal who has a reputation for dealing with tough situations, a fellow by the name of Jake Timber. But the governor's worried that this might be too much for one man, even one of his caliber so he's asking me to send someone south to Palestine to join up with him.

Bass looked confused. "Why're you tellin' *me* marshal?

"All my deputies are tied up right now Bass," said Mudd. "But, Marshal Fagan speaks very highly of you. Him 'n Judge Parker both say you're one of their best. I asked yesterday if I could have your services for a spell 'n Fagan got back to me this morning approvin' it.

"Uh, you want me to go work with this here Timber fella?" It was the last thing *he* wanted to do, but he would obey instructions

"Yeah. I know you wanted to go home to see your wife 'n young 'uns . . . how many ya got now?

"Last time I counted there was six, but Nellie's already big with another one.

"Dang man, I hope ya have a big house."

"It's big enough," Bass said. "Got me a farm in Van Buren, jest a few miles northeast of Fort Smith. Lotta room to expand."

"Well I hate like the dickens to do this to ya, 'cause I know ya want to go home but the governor wants an extra man 'n you're all I got right now."

Bass sighed. "Okay, when do you want me in Palestine?"

"It's a four-day ride or ya could take the stage over to Longview 'n take a train from there. That'd save ya two days maybe so long as the train don't break down."

Bass stood. "Okay, marshal," he said. "I'll be in Palestine in four days."

XXXXX

FROM MUDD'S office Bass had gone on to his little sleeping cubicle and put his gear together. Then he'd gone to the marshal's support office to talk to the clerk about drawing some advance money to cover his expenses for this unanticipated side trip

At the same time he couldn't help but wonder what was going on. He wasn't familiar with Jake Timber other than the occasional story but from what he'd heard the man was some kind of legend. Why a man of his caliber would need assistance was beyond imagining. Bass, though new at being a deputy marshal often went into Indian Territory after multiple fugitives with his Cherokee friend Henry Lone Tree and one additional posse man to drive the tumbleweed wagon and keep an eye on the outlaws they picked up and a cook and chuck wagon. He had even on one or two occasions gone after outlaws alone and other than the fact that he was known as one of the best sharpshooters in Arkansas—so good with pistol or rifle fired with either hand that he'd been barred from entering shooting competitions. He spoke six of the tribal languages of the territory and was such a good tracker that it was said that he could track a lizard across a rock. Even then he had nowhere near the reputation of this Timber character. Still, no one had ever decided that he needed help that he didn't ask for. And, he was pretty certain that Timber hadn't asked for help. He didn't sound like the kind of man who *would* ask for help. That left him feeling uneasy. He knew how he would feel if the roles were reversed and he didn't look forward to Timber's reaction to being treated like he wasn't capable of handling the job

There was, though nothing he could do about it. Orders were orders and he would no more refuse to obey instructions than he would cheat on his wife or deliberately break a Commandment, well, except for the one about 'bearing false witness'. While some took that one to mean that a person should never tell a lie Bass believed that the occasional untruth when it was for good reason was acceptable. He often used little lies to snooker outlaws into giving up and he couldn't believe that a person would be condemned to hell for that. The other nine though he took quite literally and tried his best not to break them

As he hauled his saddle bags, rifle, and necessaries bag down to the stall where his big grey stallion awaited he tried to block the negative aspects of the assignment from his mind and focus on the possibilities

The marshal had mentioned a gang, so he imagined at least four outlaws, probably more and figured them to be bank or stagecoach robbers. If they'd been cattle rustlers he felt sure the marshal would've mentioned it. Texans and rustlers, cattle or horse had a long and colorful relationship. For a long time and even down to the present he knew Texans had dealt with rustlers on their own and summarily usually by escorting them to the nearest low limb where they arranged for a long drop at the end of a short rope. Even the stories that Texas Rangers had been known early in their history to dispense summary justice to rustlers and murderers. It wasn't the case anymore, or not as much and especially not where the marshals were involved. Some who wore the badge of marshal or deputy had come from the shady side of the line but not many and the new crop of judges like Isaac Parker, his judge back in Arkansas were sticklers for not only enforcing but obeying the law

As he saddled his horse and tied the bags to the saddle he'd pretty much formed a picture in his mind of what was to come, a picture that he knew was pure fantasy but it gave him something to think about other than the probable rocky relationship he'd have with his new partner

His imaginings would undergo several transformations during the four-day ride, but one thing wouldn't change. Whether his relationship with Timber was good or bad he would do his utmost to uphold the honor of the U.S. Marshal Service.

5

BEFORE AND AFTER every robbery the Farnum Gang always met in an abandoned farmhouse in Northeast Texas, five miles south of the Oklahoma border. Two days after they freed Butch Farnum and killed Joe Don Horton the gang members were at the farmhouse where Butch was divvying up the proceeds of their last two robberies. The big outlaw was fierce and mean as they com, but in an odd way he was a fair man. Most gang leaders took the lion's share of their ill-gotten gains and split the leavings amongst the rest of the men. Butch split the take evenly among everybody in the gang. He kept the same amount as the rest. He felt like it was the best way to keep men loyal and he was right. Men rode with him until they made one mistake too many or got killed in a hold-up. When that happened Butch always made sure the dead man's part of the haul reached his next of kin.

Finishing the distribution of money, watches, and jewelry stolen while freeing him the leader proposed a toast

"Wait a minute, Butch," said Ollie. "You, you didn't give me no money."

"You big tub of guts," said Butch, "I pay the ones who do their job. The last time we took you on a caper you caused me to get caught and damn near got me killed. I was damn lucky I didn't break my neck when you turned loose of my horse too soon and I fell." He walked over to his older brother. "Stand up, Fat."

Reluctantly, Ollie did as he was told. He started to speak when Butch slapped him hard with the back of his hand. The mentally challenged man fell to his knees and began to sob

"If you don't shut up that bawlin', Ollie, I'm gonna hit you again. Get up."

The frightened man got on his hands and knees then stood on shaky legs. He held his arms in front of his face afraid his brother would hit him again.

Butch reached down and brushed dirt from Ollie's pants then put his hands on the portly man's shoulders. "Ollie," he said, "you know I don't enjoy hittin' you, but you got to understand this is a business we're in and a business is only as good as its weakest link." He rubbed tears from his brother's eyes. "I know it ain't easy for you to think, big brother, but you have to try harder. Okay?" Ollie nodded. Butch dug in his pocket and came up with twenty-dollar gold piece. Handing it to Ollie he said, "You're my brother and I ain't gonna let you starve. Now don't go spendin' all that money on beer. Save some for the saloon girls."

Ollie managed a weak smile. "Thank you, Butch." He hugged his brother.

Butch pushed him away. "Next time you go to town take a bath Ollie. You smell like horse shit." He turned to Chance. "Brother, I'm countin' on you to make sure Ollie gets a bath."

"I'll do that boss," said Chance. "Ollie tomorrow we'll ride down to Paris and get a couple of beers and you can get cleaned up all nice and purty"

The youngest Farnum brother laughed.

Butch stared a hole through the young man. "You got somethin' to say, Little Willie?"

Wille Bob lowered his eyes. "No sir, but don't call me Little Willie. You know I don't like that name."

"Then act like a man and respect your elders. Unless you want to take a shot at takin' over the gang?"

Willie Bob shook his head stood up and walked outside

"All right y'all, let's get some sleep. I'll meet you here in thirty days with a new plan. Good night."

XXXXX

BEFORE SETTLING in for the night Wade Morgan and Erastus Franks stepped outside for a cigarette. Morgan lighted a quirly, sucked in a lungful of acrid smoke and exhaled through his nose.

"If it was me," he said, "I'd shoot that fat bastard, Ollie, and be done with it. He ain't worth a pinch of shit. Little Willie needs to be taken down a notch too. He thinks he's hot stuff with a gun. Hell, I could let him draw first and still beat him. Who knows? Maybe someday I'll prod him enough that he'll draw on me."

Franks threw down the cigarette he had been smoking. "You do that and Butch'll put out your candle real quick

"I ain't afraid of Mr. Butch Farnum. I ain't afraid of nobody."

"The man who ain't afraid of no one is a fool or just plain stupid or maybe a little bit of both." Franks strode into the house.

Morgan eased his hand down to the butt of his gun, "You ain't too big to cut down neither, black man," he said, careful not to say it loud enough for Erastus Franks to hear.

6

TIMBER CHECKED his room out and he was pleased to have a window facing the street. Looking out he had a good view up and down. It was busy out there but it may quieten down later. He wondered where Bass Reeves was and when he might show up? Whatever, he would wait for him but if he was too long Timber resolved to start work on his own and join up with the deputy marshal later.

It was early evening and Timber needed somewhere to stable Scout for the night. He went back down to the lobby and up to the desk where the same clerk was writing in a book at the desk.

"You got a livery stable close to here?" Timber asked.

The clerk looked up at him, "Yes we do and a mighty fine one it is too if I may say so."

Timber figured that he already had, "So where is it?"

The clerk was taken short but he didn't show his frustration, "Turn left out of the hotel to the bottom of the street. Then turn left again, can't miss it down the left-hand side."

Timber thanked him and went out to Scout, then he rode him down to the stable. He found it easily enough as he had been told and rode Scout inside where he dismounted. It was a large barn with two big doors. Inside it was pretty good as the clerk had said. There were stalls running down both sides of a central walkway and room for wagons and such at the end. As he looked round a man came walking up to him.

"Can I help you?" He asked as he got close.

"Yeah I need stabling and feed for my horse."

"Well you've come to the right place sure enough," the hostler was tall and friendly, he gave Timber a wide smile. "Just the one night?" He asked.

"Maybe, maybe not."

"I got me plenty of room. You can leave him here as long as you want and pick him up when you're ready, pay up when you leave."

Timber agreed to leave Scout there for the night not knowing how long he would need him stabled. Hopefully he would meet up with the deputy marshal by tomorrow and make a decision once they had talked. He took Scout to the stall offered him and took his saddle off. It was a fine stable and there were places for everything. Once he was happy and rubbed Scout down he left him and walked out. It was a short walk back to the hotel where he checked again if Bass Reeves had arrived. He hadn't.

With time to kill Timber took a walk to discover just what business and buildings there were in the streets around him. He passed a restaurant he liked the look of and called in to eat. The steak was good and hung off the plate which he had with potatoes and gravy. He washed it down with a few cups of coffee then wandered around some more. He was here to meet Bass Reeves and then the two of them were to track down and apprehend a band of outlaws led by a Butch Farnum, now what more could he find out to help that? As it was he had no idea. Maybe Bass would have more information for him? He walked back to the hotel, got a bath and spent a night in a soft bed.

The next morning he was up early as he always was, dressed and down to the lobby. It was too early to ask about Bass Reeves again and anyway the clerk was fed up of him asking. Every time he glanced across at him the clerk shook his head. Where was that man?

With Bass still not around and no one to ask for information he decided to find a sheriff's office and see if he had any information for him. He walked back to the desk clerk.

"He hasn't registered yet marshal," the clerk said to him.

Timber stopped and gave him a little grin, "Where will I find the sheriff's office?"

The clerk sighed and explained to him where it was. It sounded a little way so Timber went to get Scout. The horse was pleased to see him and accepted the carrot Timber had picked up along the way for him. Once he was saddled up Timber led him out of the stall and went to find the hostler who was working on filling feed bins to one side at the end of the barn.

"Going already?" The hostler asked.

"For today yeah. I'll be back later. What do I owe you?"

Timber paid the fee and then mounted up and rode out. The sheriff's office was in Courthouse Square and he had clear instructions on how to find it. Minutes later he pulled up outside, he looped Scout's reins over the rail and stepped up to the office. It was one of the fanciest offices he'd ever seen. He got to the door and walked in. He was met with a large room with a desk, chairs, cabinets and rifle racks. At the back he could see an open door that led through to the cells. There was no one there so Timber called out to have a head peer around the cell door at him.

"Be right with you," the man said.

Timber waited until the sheriff came out to him, "Now what can I do for you?"

Timber pulled his marshal badge for a pocket and held it out, "Marshal Jake Timber. I'm looking for some information."

"Information? Well marshal, I'm sheriff Emery Wilson, you go ahead." Wilson was bemused by the sight of the man standing in front of him. It wasn't every day a marshal wearing deerskins came in to see him.

"I'm here to look into a gang of outlaws that have been causing mayhem in the area they are led by a Butch Farnum. Does that mean anything to you?"

"The Farnum gang. Yeah I've heard of them. They are brothers, not sure how many and they recruit others to work with them when needed. They appear and disappear, sure can't seem to get a handle on any of them."

"You have any wanted notices on them?"

"Well let's see now," Wilson strode over to a cabinet, pulled open a drawer and began looking through a pile of paper. "I have one here for Butch Farnum and one for Chance Farnum but that's it."

Timber took them off him and studied the pictures.

"I need to keep these, where was their last hit?"

"They stopped a train a few days back, killed the fireman and robbed all the passengers. Here I'll show you."

Wilson went to a map on the wall and prodded it with a stubby finger, "Right here."

Timber studied the location and nodded, "Okay that's a start I guess."

"You going after them boys?"

"Yeah."

"A tall order for one man."

"Oh I won't be alone. I'm waiting on a deputy marshal to help me out," Timber touched his hat and walked out. He spent most of the day trying to get more information. He checked in at two newspaper offices and got some more detail to go with what he already knew. He ate at the same restaurant and spent another night in the hotel with Scout in the livery stable. The governor had told him to wait for deputy marshal Reeves to arrive so that was what he was going to do.

It wasn't until Timber had taken breakfast the following morning and walked around until midday that he checked in again at the hotel. The clerk was pleased to tell him that Bass Reeves had in fact arrived and checked in.

7

BASS HAD ESTIMATED the time it would take him to ride from Paris to Palestine correctly almost to the hour. He'd also been correct in his belief that accommodations along the way would be scarce. He had found a small boarding house belonging to a black couple in the town of Mineola, at about the halfway point in the journey. For the remaining three nights he'd slept under the stars in whatever convenient clearing he found not that he objected to that. In many ways because of the muggy atmosphere even late into the evening of East Texas, it was more comfortable outside than inside a structure where the hot air was trapped and draped itself over a person at night like a wool blanket.

The only problem was the mosquitoes and on occasion, the bats. He solved that by building a good fire that kept most animals at bay in the early hours and the smoke helped with the mosquitoes later when the fire died down

Finally, near midday of the fourth day he had arrived in Palestine, a town that was experiencing something of a boom with the arrival of the railroad. One of the streets he rode down in his search for the hotel where he was supposed to meet Timber he saw a number of fancy mansions that clearly belonged to some mighty wealthy people. Paris had nothing like it.

The hotel wasn't quite as fancy as the mansions he'd passed but it beat the little space he'd had to sleep in in Paris, and to his surprise the white clerk didn't bat an eye when he walked in, identified himself and asked to rent a room.

"Marshal Timber's been asking me every hour it seems when you'd get here," the clerk said

"Is he 'round?" Bass asked.

"No you just missed him but he should be back shortly." The clerk pushed the register toward him.

Bass winced. "You mind writin' my name for me?" he said. "I can make my X, but I don't read or write so good."

The clerk looked surprised but held his tongue. He picked up the pen and wrote 'Bass Reeves' on the first blank line immediately beneath Timber's name. Bass nodded his thanks and took the key.

He went to his room and stored his saddle bags and rifle, then back to the lobby where he got directions to the livery stable. He rode his grey stallion there and arranged for a stall then walked back to the hotel. With nothing else to do he decided to wait in the lobby for the marshal.

His wait wasn't long. Even though no one had ever described Timber to him he instantly recognized him when he walked into the lobby. As tall as Bass's six-two he had green eyes that looked as hard as green gemstones to Bass and a way of walking that suggested a man of action who was constantly prepared for whatever might come his way

The man went straight for the desk clerk. Bass got up and walked toward him. As he drew near he heard the man say, "Any idea where he is now?"

"I'm right behind you."

Timber turned around surprised to hear the deep tone of voice behind him. They stood eyeball to eyeball which was a new experience for Bass him being a tad taller than the average man. He stuck out his hand. "I'm Bass Reeves, you must be Jake Timber," he said.

Timber's handshake was firm no nonsense even though the fingers were gnarled. Bass looked straight at him waiting for an answer.

"Yeah, I'm Timber. You took your time getting here."

The man was blunt almost impolite Bass felt. And it appeared that he wanted to be called by his last name. *If that's the way he wants it that's fine by me.* "It's been a four-day ride. I'm here now so maybe we'd better get acquainted."

Timber didn't seem to be put off by Bass being blunt with him so Bass just put it down to that being the way he was.

Timber's tummy was rumbling so he figured the best way to get acquainted was go eat with the deputy marshal and talk. He took Bass to the restaurant he'd been using and they found a table which sat right well with Bass. Except for one meal in the boarding house in Mineola, he'd eaten trail rations and not having a posse cook with him made a big difference in the way his meals tasted. He had to admit he wasn't the best trail cook in the world.

The place they went to was a bit on the fancy side unlike the places in Indian Territory where Bass and his friend Henry Lone Tree usually ate when they weren't eating the grub prepared by whichever cook had been assigned to him.

"This place is a bit grand. Timber," Bass said as they sat. "I hope it's on your account?"

"I ain't got no account, Reeves," Timber responded. "But don't worry. I'll be picking up the tab."

The waitress was young and an outgoing type who smiled a lot but Bass was more interested in the food. He ordered a steak with everything. Timber also ordered steak. As they waited for the food and then after it arrived Bass wanted Timber to explain to him what he was doing in Palestine when he should be back home in Van Buren with his family enjoying some overdue time off. Timber though seemed about as talkative as an oak tree so Bass decided it would be up to him.

"Any idea why the governor wants both of us on this job, Timber?" he asked.

Timber shrugged. "Beats me. I was kinda hoping you'd tell me."

Well, that didn't work. Getting Timber to talk was like pulling teeth. Bass gave up and concentrated on the food which was delicious. When they'd finished their steaks and sat back Timber gave him a very brief version of what he knew, brief almost to the point of nothingness.

Then the waitress came back to the table. She was keen to serve the men as Timber had been a good tipper the times she had seen him.

"Will that be all or can I tempt you with some apple pie? I've heard it's very good," she said.

"Yeah sure," said Bass, "bring some over."

The waitress looked down and seemed to notice for the first time the badge that Bass wore on his chest. "You're in town to work?" she asked.

Timber took a badge from his pocket and pinned it to his shirt.

"We both are," he said.

"After anyone special?" The waitress was a naturally nosy person and her job gave her plenty to nosy into.

"Actually yes we are," said Bass. "You heard of the Farnum Gang?"

"The Farnum's? Are you really after them, just the two of you?"

Bass noticed Timber's frown and wondered if he'd somehow overstepped by bringing their mission up to the waitress.

Timber had heard that comment before today, "Yeah we are, so what can you tell us?" He asked in a tone that implied that he suspected she knew something important.

The waitress, who had introduced herself as Annie Cole when she came to their table to take their order looked around nervously. Then she leaned in close and lowered her voice. "There's a girl who works as a waitress at Lester's Dance Palace. You could ask her," she said in a voice not much above a whisper.

"This waitress have a name?" Timber asked curtly.

"Scarlett. I don't know her last name. Word is she's hot on Chance Farnum.

Timber looked pointedly at Bass.

"Sounds good Timber," Bass said.

"Yeah, I guess we need to go there, but after that apple pie," said Timber.

Bass smiled. Curt he might be but Timber had his priorities straight.

After they finished the pie Timber put several crumpled banknotes on the table more than was needed for the bill then he asked the waitress for directions to Lester's and took off his badge. He nodded at Bass's. "No sense in us advertising things," he said.

Bass removed his badge and put it in the inside pocket of his jacket. This he understood. He often removed his badge and rumpled his clothing when entering places for the first time. No sense spooking people by letting them know right off that he was the law.

Lester's Dance Palace was big swell place, gaudy, and loud. They were stopped at the door by a mountain of a man dressed in a black suit and carrying a .45 caliber Smith & Wesson in a fancy black leather holster. He had his arms folded across his massive chest.

"We have rules gents. Patrons must be dressed in decent clothes, not smell bad because the ladies don't like it, can't be drunk, and have money.

Bass was still wearing what he'd worn on the trail, and hadn't bathed in two days. He had also left most of his travel money in his hotel room. The only one of the rules he figured he was okay on was the part about being sober.

"Looks like we failed on two counts," Bass said to Timber.

Timber though didn't seem one bit fazed. He looked up at the big man.

"Okay, we may look bad, we may smell bad, but boy have we got money," he said. Timber was speaking for himself not knowing how much Bass had.

"That's one out of three anyways," the man hesitated. He didn't seem impressed and mumbled something that Bass didn't catch then he heard him say, "My big brother may not like me letting you in."

"Who's your brother?" asked Bass.

The big man smiled at him. "Only the owner of the place, Lester," he said.

"Well," Bass said. "If you're family then maybe you could persuade him to let two wealthy men into the place." the man frowned at him, then burst out laughing. "I guess I could at that," he said.

Timber was smiling at Bass as they walked into the place.

They went directly to the bar near the back of the crowded room. The bartender ignored them until Timber pulled some banknotes from his pocket then as quick as a jackrabbit, he was in front of them.

"What can I get ya, gents?" he asked.

Timber ordered two beers without asking Bass what he wanted. Bass shrugged. As long as Timber was paying he didn't mind. He wasn't planning on doing more than taking a sip anyway. As the bartender brought the drinks. Timber leaned in close to him.

"I hear you have a dancer here named Scarlett?" he said.

The bartender beamed. "That we do, sir," he said. "Scarlett's the most popular and I might add the most beautiful dancer in this place and she'll dance with anybody who has the money . . . well, except when Chance Farnum's here. Chance considers Scarlett his property. He's real jealous and a stone-cold killer. Any man he sees dancin' with her he challenges to a gunfight 'n he's fast Chance is. If you want to see Scarlett you need to come back late tonight. That's when she's workin'. Chance might not be here tonight." He shrugged.

Timber threw back his drink. Bass took a sip of his and put the glass on the bar.

"Then I reckon we'll come back after supper," said Timber.

Bass followed him out of the place and they walked back to the hotel. When they arrived Bass said, "I think maybe we oughta bathe 'n change into some more presentable clothes before we go back, don't you?"

Timber shrugged. "If you say so," he said. Timber didn't have much in the way of clean clothes but he did rinse through what he had and hung them to dry in his room before going out.

Bass and Timber met up in the lobby of the hotel and went to the hotel's small restaurant where they had supper. After finishing their meal they walked to Lester's. The place was even more crowded and noisy than it had been earlier. The big man at the door recognized them and the fact that they'd washed and changed into slightly more presentable clothes, well at least one of them had he waved them in.

They walked through the crowded room where cowboys, loggers, and an assortment of other men were lined up clutching banknotes waiting their turn to dance with one of the fourteen pretty women in frilly flared dresses. Bass and Timber went to the bar.

"What'll it be gentlemen?" the bartender asked, a different man than the one who'd been behind the bar when they came in earlier.

"Two beers," Timber said. "And we're looking for Scarlett. I hear she's your most popular dancer."

As he poured their beer the bartender grinned broadly. "That's for sure," he said, pointing at a tall woman with rusty-red hair piled atop her head. She wore a red dress that was pleated and flared and ended just above her ankles and was the one of the fourteen women who had the longest line of men waiting for a chance to swing her across the dance floor.

Bass could see that the woman was attractive and she was certainly a good dancer but he'd never understood why men made such a fuss over dancing with a woman who didn't even know your name and even if you told her she'd forget it by the time she'd danced with fifteen or twenty other men. He much preferred dancing with his darling Nellie and they didn't need the music of a tinny piano in a place so noisy you could hardly hear it. He glanced at Timber at his side who seemed similarly unaffected.

The two of them stood with their backs to the bar watching the dance floor, in particular the redhead who moved effortlessly from man to man with a fixed smile on her face and sipped their beers.

Scarlett was being swung across the floor with a young man whose muscular build and work-roughened hands marked as a logger when the line of men waiting for her suddenly shifted to some of the other girls. Standing in their place was a man only slightly smaller than the bouncer wearing a fancy brown suit with a derby set at a rakish angle on his head. He was a slick looking dandy whose handsomeness was marred by the murderous scowl on his face

The young logger didn't notice at first but the nervous looks on the men dancing with women near him and the way they moved their dance partners away from him must have signaled that something was amiss. He stopped dancing and looked around. When he saw Chance Farnum standing at the edge of the dance floor with a murderous look in his eyes his face turned as pale as new parchment. He let Scarlett's left hand drop from his right hand and removed his right hand from her shoulder. At first he was frozen in place like a deer that's suddenly been cornered. Then he looked around. The other dancers and their partners had cleared a large space around him which included a path to the front door of the dance parlor. The young man made an instant and in Bass's opinion, wise decision. He cut and run toward the door as fast as his legs could carry him never looking back.

Scarlett scowled at Chance. "Dagnabbit it Chance," she said. "How am I supposed to make a living if you keep scaring customers off like that?"

He looked down at her, hands on his hips and an arrogant smile on his face. "Well now, Miss Scarlett," he said coldly. "I thought you were my girl. Am I gonna have to find myself a new girlfriend?"

There was something menacing in his voice. Even Bass picked up on it. So did Scarlett. Her eyes widened and her face was obviously pale under the layer of heavy makeup she wore. As she approached him her lips trembled.

"Awe Chance, you know I was just joshing," she said in a quivering voice. "I'm sorry. Can you forgive me?"

He smirks at her. "Yeah, I forgive you . . . this time. C'mere 'n let's dance."

As she meekly let him lead her back onto the dance floor Bass heard Timber snort next to him.

"This is neither the place nor the time to take this hombre," Timber said. Bass couldn't make out how the marshal was feeling.

His voice was even, but his jaws seemed tight. "Let's go chin wag on what would be a better place."

Bass shrugged and followed Timber as he headed for the door. He didn't know what was on the marshal's mind but he was frankly happy to be leaving such a noisy place.

8

THEY WALKED BACK to the hotel in silence and upon arrival retired to their rooms. By pure coincidence they were up and in the hotel's restaurant at about the same time the next morning and while eating Timber suggested that they ride out to the woods around Palestine to see if they could find any likely hideouts. He had the restaurant's cook prepare food for them both, fried chicken, corn on the cob, and biscuits, which wouldn't require much effort and could even be eaten while riding if they desired.

The land around the town was mostly gently rolling hills covered mostly in pine trees with a few stands of oak, maple, and a few wild chinaberry trees from seeds that had been scattered by birds as these ornamental trees were commonly planted around plantation houses in the south. The hills and meadows were cut in places by sluggish creeks and expanses of swamp where cypress was the predominant tree. There were a number of places that would've been suitable hideouts but they saw no signs of recent use.

At midday they stopped and tethered the horses to a cypress on the banks of a stream that flowed in a snakelike course across a flat expanse that was part meadow, part marsh. They found a solid spot on the banks of the stream and Timber gathered wood and made a fire while Bass fashioned a rack from some fallen branches to hang the coffee pot from. Soon, the smell of brewing coffee mixed in with the slightly sweet scent of honeysuckle.

When the coffee was just right Bass filled two tin cups and handed one to Timber. They took the oil cloth bundles of food from their saddle bags and sat cross-legged eating and looking at the gently undulating surface of the stream that was so shallow they could see tadpoles darting about near the bank.

"You ever think about turning in your badge and buying a little place on land like this Bass?"

Bass had become so accustomed to Timber's curt, taciturn nature that at first he missed what he'd said. Then he realized that this was Timber making polite conversation. Bass smiled. He'd picked one doozy of a subject to chin wag about. Bass had a conflicted relationship with Texas. On the one hand it was where he'd met his wife, Nellie, the love of his life but on the other it was where he'd been taken against his will when he was eight and then when he was nearly thirty taken into combat by the eldest son of his former owner - Bass steadfastly refused to even think of William Reeves as his master or any other man for that matter - George from whom he'd run away to Indian Territory until the war ended and slavery had been finally outlawed throughout the land.

"I already got me a farm," he said. "In Van Buren, Arkansas. Finest piece of land you ever seen too."

"Yeah, but don't you find the land here . . . pleasing?"

Bass looked around. "It's got places that ain't bad," he said. "But I'd rather be in a place that don't have so many snakes, scorpions and bats as here. Plus I don't know if you noticed, but the weather here ain't exactly welcomin'. In the summer it's so hot you have a hard time sleepin' at night 'n in the winter it rains 'n gets all muddy 'n that red mud gets into everything."

Timber smiled. "I take that to mean you don't plan on retiring down here."

Bass returned the smile. "You take it right. Arkansas . . . or maybe

Indian Territory. Places with proper hills and no swamps. That's where I'll hang my hat."

"Every man to himself," said Timber. "I kinda like it here. The peace and quiet. Ain't no place perfect but this comes close in my book."

Bass didn't want to insult the man so he just nodded. "Say, did you learn what you needed to know watchin' that Chance Farnum fella last night?"

Timber stared off into the distance for several seconds. Then, he removed his hat and ran his hand through his hair. A few seconds of that and then he looked at Bass and nodded. "Yeah, I did," he said. "We'll take him tonight."

Bass nodded at that and as Timber didn't say anything else he just finished his coffee.

They looked around the area some more and mutually agreed that there was just too much territory to find anything this way, so they rode back to town and when they reached the hotel they agreed that they would go to Lester's around eight.

They had supper at the hotel and arrived at Lester's a few minutes past eight. When they entered they immediately saw Scarlett dancing with a young ranch hand so they knew that Chance Farnum wasn't there yet. They went to the bar ordered two beers which they let sit there as they stood with their backs to the bar and surveyed the room.

The wait wasn't long. The first sign that something was amiss was when one of the women who'd been dancing near the entrance pulled away from her partner, ran to Scarlett and whispered something in her ear. Scarlett's eyes grew wide and she said something to the man she was dancing with. His face turned pale and he fairly ran away from her to get into line for one of the other dancers. Scarlett walked to the wall and waited with her head down.

Chance Farnum strolled into the place as if he owned it and went straight to her. He took her hand and pulled her out onto the dance floor and began dancing. Bass could see that she looked miserable whenever Chance couldn't see her face but smiled weakly when he could.

"Well," he said to Timber. "There he is. How're we gonna take him?"

"I've been cogitating on that, Bass," Timber said. "Seeing as how he's so possessive of Scarlett and all I'd think the way to get him outside would be to make a move on her. You dance?"

Bass shook his head. "Only with my Nellie 'n only when we're at home when ain't nobody else lookin'. What about you?"

"Shoot, I ain't no dancer neither." Then Timber snapped his fingers. "But there just might be a way to get his attention without having to dance. I reckon he's got a pretty big ego. Watch my back while I go see if I can prick it."

Bass had no idea what Timber was up to, but he patted his jacket which was concealing his .44. Timber likewise was wearing his shirt low over his revolvers.

Timber walked to the edge of the dance floor.

"Hey, friend," he said pointing so that Chance would know who he was talking to. "Why don't you sit down and let the lady dance with somebody who knows how to dance. I've seen crippled cows dance better than you."

Chance stopped and pushed Scarlett away.

"You talkin' to me mister?" he asked in a menacing tone.

"I don't see anybody else out on that floor with two left feet," said Timber.

"You got a death wish friend? You either apologize or get yourself ready to meet your maker."

"I only apologize when I'm wrong," Timber said. "And what I just said about you is just the natural truth."

"That's it. Outside. You and me," Chance snapped.

"P-please don't Chance," Scarlett pleaded. "He's new in town and doesn't know your rules."

"Don't matter. I'll tell him my rules just before I kill him. Now, you go stand over there and be quiet. I'll take care of you as soon as I kill this hombre."

He pushed her toward the wall and walked toward the door turning his back on Timber with a disdainful look on his face.

Timber followed about six feet behind him, and Bass walked behind him, keeping an eye on the other men in the place. But no one did anything but stare.

When Timber reached the door just seconds after Chance had barreled through it the big bouncer who'd greeted them stepped in front of him and leaned in close.

"Mister," he said. "My name's Noah like the old fella that built the ark. You got some grit going up against Chance Farnum. Watch 'im. He likes to talk to try to distract you and then he'll draw down on you. If you're lucky and you take him I'll buy you a glass of whatever it is you're drinking."

Timber nodded curtly and walked past him. The big bouncer looked worried. Bass pushed past him.

Outside he saw that Timber had stepped into the street and was facing Chance who stood about ten feet away with his feet apart and his arms at his side.

Timber pulled his shirt up to show his guns. Just as the bouncer had warned Chance started nattering.

"Mister before I kill you," he said. "You oughta know why I'm doing it. Scarlett's my woman and ain't no other man allowed to lay a hand on her. Likewise ain't nobody can get away with insulting me and stay on the right side of the grass. I hope you're getting this so it's the last thing you remember."

Timber stood silent.

Chance opened his mouth as if to say something else and at the same time thrust his hand down and started drawing his weapon. Bass put his hand near his jacket's flap, just in case.

Chance was a hair's breadth faster than Timber on the draw but like most people he didn't realize that a hand weapon is notoriously inaccurate even up close and if you're too fast you're likely to miss the first shot especially if you try aiming. Timber on the other hand was as calm as a rock formation. Not fast but steady and deliberate. He whipped out his sidearm and brought it up but instead of trying to aim he merely pointed and pulled the trigger a heartbeat before Chance could aim and pull his.

Timber's slug caught the outlaw in the center of the chest. He twitched as the lead buried itself deep in his heart, dead before his brain even knew his heart had stopped beating. He took a single step backwards, his eyes rolled back in the sockets and he dropped to his knees and then fell forward face down in the dusty street his limp fingers still holding his unfired revolver limply. A large dark spot began to grow from beneath his upper torso.

The street was quiet. People crowded in the door of Lester's and stared at the dead outlaw. Scarlett pushed through the crowd and stood over the body looking down at it for a few seconds. Then she hawked a big glob of spit at him and turned back to Timber and Bass who stood side by side at the edge of the boardwalk.

"Thank you, mister," she said to Timber thrusting out a hand. He shook it. "You just done me the biggest favor anybody ever did. Chance was kinda nice to me when other folks were looking but in private he beat me . . . all the time. He'd hit me where it wouldn't show. He was a pure evil man and if you hadn't killed him I think he would've killed me tonight. From now on anytime you want to dance you dance with me and you don't have to pay."

"I'm glad I was able to help you, Miss Scarlett," Timber said. "I might take you up on that invite but not tonight if you don't mind."

She smiled in return to Timber's and patted his shoulder. As she turned to go back into Lester's the big bouncer approached Timber and Bass.

"Hell fire, man," he said. "That was some shooting you did. Hey, some of you boys get Chance over to the undertakers." While two men rushed down to drag the dead outlaw away, the bouncer put his hands around Timber and Bass's shoulders.

"The two of you c'mon back inside with me. I think instead of one glass the rest of your drinks this evening are on the house."

Bass had seen gun fights before. Had even been in a few himself. This kind of face-off in the middle of the street though was new to him. Timber on the other hand seemed to take it in stride. What Bass did know now though was that Timber had thrown the gauntlet. The Farnum gang had been put on notice.

Timber didn't seem excited or concerned about that and if he wasn't neither would Bass be.

The three men were laughing as they walked back into the dance parlor.

9

"I HAVE to thank you for taking out that loser. Chance Farnum has been a pain in my side ever since he started coming in here now I don't have to bother with him no more," Noah said as they got inside.

"Always glad to help," Timber said.

"I often thought of taking him out myself but although I'm gun savvy I'd have been no match for him. You did good, you just let me know anytime you need me. Just send me a message and I'll be there."

"As it is you can help us some more Noah," Bass asked him, "Do you know anything about the rest of the Farnum gang or anything about any one of them?"

Noah stopped and rubbed his chin, "As I recall there is one of the gang, Jimmy Littlejohn who has a small farm over in Jacksonville."

Timber and Bass nodded their heads and Bass asked for more information.

"Yeah well there are five Littlejohn brothers, each one of them meaner than the last. They have a sister too; Felicity is her name. Lavelle is the eldest one of them, maybe the meanest. From what I hear he sure runs that family."

"Thanks Noah that's all good to know," Timber told him.

Noah was on a roll and carried on talking, "Watch out for Jimmy, he is tall with long shoulder length blonde hair and no facial hair. He is supposed to be fearless. Another thing you should know is that Felicity is or rather was sweet on Chance Farnum."

"You're just a mine of information when you open up Noah," Bass said to him.

"If you intend to go out there I can tell you that the train for Jacksonville leaves at eight am every morning."

Bass thanked him and he turned to leave the dance hall with Timber right beside him.

When they were outside Bass could tell that Timber was deep in thought, "A dime for them?" He asked.

"I've been thinking. I might be an idea for us to tell that Felicity that Chance is dead, maybe not who by, not immediately anyways. Maybe that will make her go to pieces and say things she might not otherwise come out with."

"Sounds good to me Timber, we can try that."

"That will probably be a good time for us then to make our play."

They walked off and back towards the hotel where they stopped off for supper at a cafe on the way to talk more on the Farnum gang.

"What do you reckon Timber, just how many are there in this gang we're up against?"

"Well now let's see. We know there are four Farnum brothers and five Littlejohn's so that's nine we know of, well eight now."

"But they bring in others as they need them," Bass commented.

"Yeah so we been told. I guess it will be hard to know who they are until they turn up if they do?"

Bass thought on that, "Maybe once we make our play they'll all come out of the woodwork."

"Maybe so then we can eliminate the vermin as we see them."

"I hope it goes down that way," Bass said with a meaningful look.

They spent the night in the hotel and got ready the next morning to move out. Both men were up at dawn and out at the cafe for breakfast soon after. Then it was a walk to the livery stable for their horses and off to the railroad station. They got tickets easily enough and loaded their horses into a stock car. Then it was a case of finding seats in a passenger car for the journey out to Jacksonville.

10

THE TRAIN JOURNEY went by peacefully enough and it pulled into Jacksonville on time just an hour later. They collected their horses from the stock car and rode out into the town.

"All we gotta do now Timber is find the Littlejohn farm. You got any ideas on that?" Bass asked as they rode along.

"I usually find a trip to the sheriff's office can provide what information I need."

"That suits me but we gotta find that now?" Bass flashed his white smile over at Timber.

Getting directions to the sheriff's office was easy enough from men they met riding towards them so they carried on into the town to get to it.

They found it easily enough and as they walked in they found that it was quite busy in there with three men waiting to be served. Timber strode over to where a deputy was busy looking through a book for one of the men.

"Can you tell me where I might find the Littlejohn farm?" He interrupted him.

The deputy looked up at him, he was obviously harassed and just said, "Go south outta town you'll cross a creek over a wooden bridge. Follow the rail about two miles to a fork. Go left, can't miss it."

Timber thanked him and ushered Bass out in front of him. Once outside Timber said, "The least we have to tell the law here the better, for now anyways."

"So you going out there now Timber, my throat is parched."

"So's mine Bass. The nearest saloon first I guess."

Bass was happy with that and led the way to one just far enough away from the sheriff's office. Inside they ordered beer and found a table then began to discuss how they were going to tackle the Littlejohn place. Bass wasn't normally a drinking man but he sipped at his beer to clear his throat.

"We don't know for sure just how many of them there will be at this here farm," Bass then said.

"No we don't so we need to take some precautions. Plan for the worst, hope for the best."

"We could just ride over there and observe for a spell?"

"We could Bass but I reckon on one of us going over to the farmhouse and having a talk with them."

"One of us?"

"Yeah, I figure that will be safer. I'll go in and you find yourself a good spot where you can hole up with your rifle to cover me?"

Bass wasn't averse to that suggestion, "Okay yeah we can play it that way I guess."

"Okay, like you say though Bass we don't know the layout of the place so I guess we do need to get close up to it before we can work out our positions and timings."

"I guess we do at that."

"Okay well we know where to go but as far as we can let's keep off the trails, we don't want a few of those brothers coming along and spoiling our plan."

"Good idea, well I'm as ready as I'll ever be," Bass said taking another swallow of his beer.

Timber drained his as they stood up and went out for their horses.

Minutes later they were out of town following a dusty trail over grassland and through bunches of trees. They rode over a rise to see the creek below them with a rickety looking bridge spanning it.

"Water looks low Timber," Bass said as they stopped to take a look at it.

"Sure does, no need to use the bridge then," Timber spoke to Scout and the big horse set off on a course for the creek some way up from the bridge. Bass rode alongside him.

Getting over the creek was easy for the horses to wade through as it was shallow. Timber took a course that he figured would bring them to the fork without using the trail. It took a little longer that way but there was no worry about that.

As soon as they both saw the fork they turned their horses heads away from it on a course for the farm. They slowed down and looked about them carefully taking care to be as quiet as possible. After a few minutes they came to where they could see the farm buildings some way ahead of them. They were hidden quite well by a bunch of trees just to one side of where they were and that's where they stopped.

"Looks pretty quiet to me," Bass said.

Timber nodded without answering, then he said, "There are some trees over to the left in front of the farmhouse Bass. Do you reckon you can get there unseen?"

"You're talking to the most inconspicuous man around," Bass answered showing his pearly whites again.

Timber grinned back, "Okay you make your move, I'll wait here to watch your back while you get there then when I ride in you watch mine."

"Gotcha." Bass urged his horse back a few yards and then out around the trees to get into position. Timber watched him go and figured he couldn't have done a better job of it himself. This deputy marshal was shaping up just fine.

Once he was sure Bass was in position he spoke again to Scout and headed off for the farmhouse. He held his reins in his left hand while his right hand rested on the butt of a gun. He was in the open on the approach and although he looked very carefully he didn't see anyone there until he got up real close. Then in the shade of the porch Timber noticed a man sitting there whittling a stick. As he got closer the man put it down and stood up to greet him.

11

"Stop right there," said the man his left hand hovering over his six-shooter. "Don't even think about getting' down. If you try I'll shoot you before your foot touches the ground." The man flexed the fingers on his gun hand. "This is private property and you're tres-passin'. Turn your nag around and ride your old ass away from here."

Timber's hand rested on the butt of his .44. "I've got a message for Jimmy Littlejohn. It's about Chance Farnum."

"That right? I'm Jimmy Littlejohn. Give me the message."

"No you ain't."

"You callin' me a liar?"

Timber relaxed in his saddle, ready to make a move.

"Andy Littlejohn," a female voice said, "quit lyin' to that man and go get Jimmy. He's in the kitchen." The fellow scowled but he did what he was told.

You say you have a message from Chance?" Asked the young lady who appeared to be about twenty-five. She was pretty in a coarse sort of way with glowing green eyes and long dark red hair hanging loose around her neck. "I'm his fiancé. He's supposed to be arrivin' here any day now. Can't you tell me what he said?"

Sorry, Miss, I was paid to deliver the message to Jimmy Littlejohn. Is he around here?"

I sent Andy to get him. He'll be here in a minute." She mumbled to herself. "I wonder why Chance didn't send the message to me. I sure hope there ain't somethin' wrong.

The young man called Andy stepped out on the porch moving to the right side. A tall clean-shaven man with long blond hair followed him out and moved to the left side of the porch.

"I'm Jimmy Littlejohn. You got a message for me from Chance Farnum?"

"Y'all misunderstood me. I said I had a message about Chance Farnum, not from him."

The young lady Felicity, stepped forward. "What do you mean about him, has something happened to Chance?" She sounded like she was close to being hysterical. "What is the message? *Tell me now!*"

"A few days ago Chance Farnum was killed by a United States Marshal over in Palestine." Timber told her.

"No!" screamed Felicity dropping to her knees. Andy reached down to try and help her up but she jerked away from his touch.

"Did the Marshal shoot him in the back?" Asked Jimmy barely keeping his composure.

"They had a gunfight toe to toe in the middle of the street. I was there; I saw the whole thing. Chance started the ball but the marshal finished it. Put two slugs into Chance before he could get a shot off."

"No, no, that ain't right," said Jimmy. "My brother is the fastest man with a handgun in these parts. Stranger I think you're lyin'."

God forgive me for what I am about to do to this family. Timber looked Jimmy straight in the eye. "Maybe the marshal wasn't from these parts."

"You're a sorry liar," yelled Jimmy Littlejohn. "I'm gonna kill you." He grabbed for his gun but it wasn't even close. Timber put one slug in his throat and another in his open mouth. Before the former member of the Farnum Brother's gang hit the floor a rifle shot rang out and sent Andy flying backwards just as he was aiming his gun at Timber.

Still on her knees Felicity became silent. She looked over at her dead brother's revolver which was in easy reach of her right hand.

"Don't even think about it Miss. I ain't ever killed a woman but that don't mean I won't. Leave the gun where it is. You got dead to bury."

Felicity stood and through tear-filled eyes said, "I have three more brothers and they are the meanest ones of the bunch. When they find out what you did today they will find you and I promise as God is my witness you will beg to die before they get through with you."

An uncontrollable shiver raced up Timber's spine. "We'll be waiting in Longview." He turned his horse and kneed him into a lope. The quicker he got away from today's carnage the better he thought he would feel. He was wrong.

12

THE THREE REMAINING Littlejohn brothers rode into Longview. While the two younger brothers looked straight ahead Lavell, the oldest, kept his head on a swivel. Felicity had given him a description of Jake Timber and he was looking for the big marshal. He knew there were at least two men in on the ambush but he had no idea how many more or what they looked like. At that moment he couldn't have cared less. The big hard-featured one who killed Jimmy was meeting his maker today. The others would be found out in time and killed.

Meaner than a scorpion in heat Lavell didn't much care what had happened to Jimmy. The middle brother had been a free spirit who always chose his own path. Andy was a different story. The youngest and a sickly child growing up Lavell took him under his wing and taught the youngster everything he could about living on the fringe of the law. As he'd gotten older the youngest Littlejohn brother had gotten stronger. He was Lavell's favorite and his unforeseeable death had turned the outlaw into a revenge-seeking madman.

The brothers pulled their horses up in front of the saloon.

"We go inside," said Lavell, "and spread the word we're here to kill that *hombre* who killed our brothers. That ought to bring the rat and whoever's with him out of the woodwork." They dismounted, tied their horses to the hitching rail and walked inside. Reaching the bar Lavell ordered three beers. Turning around to look the patrons over he recognized Tad Worthington sitting alone at a table, a half-full mug of beer in front of him. The brigand sauntered over to Tad's table. "You're that Worthington kid who works for the newspaper ain't cha?"

Tad took a deep breath. "Yes sir. That is me. How may I be of service to you?"

Lavell laughed. "I'd plumb forgot how funny you talk. You must be a Yankee. I got some questions and an errand for you. How many U. S. Marshals are there in town?"

"One that I know of sir."

"He a big feller wears buckskins?"

"That's him. His name is Jake Timber."

"You know where to find him?"

"I understand he is staying at the St. Francis Hotel."

Lavell looked around the room. Besides his brothers and Tad, there were six other customers in the saloon.

"Newspaper boy I want you to go find that no good marshal and tell him the Littlejohn brothers are waitin' in the Red Rooster to kill him. You got that?"

"Yessir. May I finish my beer first?"

Lavell picked up the mug of beer and poured the contents on top of the reporter's head. "It's finished. Now git."

Tad jumped up and dashed out of the saloon. Instead of searching for Timber he beelined it towards the marshal's office.

As soon as Tad exited the Red Rooster Lavell said, "Everybody but the bartender get out of here now. There's about to be a killin'."

The place emptied out and the leader of the Littlejohn clan strode back to the bar. "Boys I have got a plan," he said to his brothers.

Barging inside the marshal's office Tad found Sheriff Tomkins sitting at his desk browsing through wanted posters. Anxious to tell the marshal what had just happened the young man burst through the door. Out of breath it took him a few moments to talk.

Seeing someone charging into his office Sheriff Tompkins

reached for his gun. Realizing who the intruder was he slid the revolver back into his holster.

"Hey there Tad why the big hurry?" Taking a moment to look the reporter over he realized Tad was soaking wet. "Boy, you smell like beer. What in blazes happened to you?" The sheriff stood and helped Tad into a chair.

Getting his breath back, Tad said, "Lavell Littlejohn and two of his brothers are in the saloon waiting for Marshal Timber. They sent me to tell him but I thought you would like to know first."

The sheriff filled a tin cup with water from a pitcher on his desk and handed it to Tad. "Drink this you'll feel better."

The frightened young man drank the water in one gulp. "I'm okay now," he said. "Should I go tell Marshal Timber?"

The lawman stood, stretched his tight muscles and hitched up his gun belt. "This is my town Tad. I will take care of this problem." Walking to a peg on the wall the marshal picked up his hat and pulled it down tight on his head. Reaching the rifle rack he opened a drawer at the bottom and fished out a handful of twelve-gauge shotgun shells. Next he drew a sawed-off Greener from the rack, broke it open and stuffed in two shells. Snapping it shut he started out of the office.

"Sheriff Tompkins," said Tad, now recovered from his mad dash, "should I tell Marshal Timber now?"

"Yes, if I don't get the job done he will have to step in." The sheriff stepped outside and headed for the saloon. Taking slow and deliberate step he cogitated on the task at hand. Figuring the three brothers would be standing apart from each other Sheriff Tompkins knew he would probably hit only one with the scattergun. That should be Lavell. Then he would drop the shotgun and draw his .45. He knew Rayford and Wayne could shoot all right but the two brothers weren't fast on the draw.

Sheriff Tompkins pushed open the swinging doors with his shotgun and stepped inside the saloon. Right away he noticed the place was empty then he realized something else. Only two of the brothers, Lavell and Rayford, stood at the counter and they were close enough together that if he fired both barrels he could hit them. He searched he place for the third brother.

"Afternoon Sheriff," said Lavell. "Come join us. We're waitin' for somebody."

The Sheriff pointed his shotgun between the two Littlejohn brothers. "Where's Wayne?" he asked using his peripheral vision to check out the saloon.

"He's right behind you Sheriff. Enjoy your nap."

Something hard hit Sheriff Tompkins above his left ear and he dropped like a two-hundred-pound sack of potatoes.

Tad Worthington found Bass and Timber in the lobby of the hotel. With bated breath he told them what was happening. The two marshals checked their guns and took off for the saloon.

Bass Reeves stopped and held up his hand. "Let's slow down and think this out. Far as we know they believe there's only one marshal. I figure the sister gave them your description but they don't know what I look like. I'm gonna walk in first like I'm just comin' in for a drink. While they're tryin' to figure out if I'm a danger to them you come in. There's three of those boys. You're the fastest so you take the two on the left and I'll take the one on the right."

Timber scowled. "Appreciate your confidence in me. I'll be sure to remember this *if* I make it through alive."

The first one to reach the saloon Bass peeked in the window. "They're spread out," he said. "One is to the right the biggest one is in the middle and another one to the left. All of 'em have got their backs to the bar. The one on the right is mine. If he goes down and I'm still standin' I'll start shootin' at the other two."

Bass took a deep breath and walked through the swinging doors. Lavell's hand dropped to his gun. "Saloon's closed," he said.

"Hey friend," said Bass, " I just come in off the trail and I need a beer to cut my thirst. Just let me have one and I'll be out of your way." The marshal started to go forward.

"One more step and you'll be out of my way for good," said Lavell. "Now get before I change my mind and shoot you where you stand."

Timber had been listening and he stepped through the doors. "Is this a private party or can I join in."

"That's him!" said Wayne. "Shoot the bastard."

Everybody went for their shooting irons. Timber cleared leather first. He shot Lavell through the heart. Swinging his .44 towards Rayford his first shot took off a piece of the man's ear. Rayford got off a shot before Timber's next round hit him in the right eye.

Bass beat his opponent to the draw and shot Wayne twice in the stomach. He turned to aid Timber but saw both brothers lying motionless on the floor.

"Good work, Bass," Timber said, holstering his gun.

"Yeah 'cept one of their bullets came a little too close and punched a hole in the side of my shirt," said Bass, sticking a finger through the new hole."

Tad Worthington strode into the room. "I was watching from the door," he said. "Darnedest thing I ever saw."

"Go get a doctor," hollered Timber.

The newspaper reporter took off like a pack of wolves were on his tail.

In ten minutes Tad returned with Doctor Julius Branford in tow. First he checked Sheriff Tompkins who was sitting in a chair holding his head. Pulling a roll of cloth from his little black bag Doctor Branford wrapped some of it around the sheriff's head, then the medic examined the Littlejohn brothers and pronounced them dead. "I purely hate it when a bunch of people get killed at the same time," said the doctor. "Now I have a whole lot of paperwork to do." He frowned and headed for his office.

13

TIMBER AND BASS searched the dead mens pockets looking for any clues they may have of other Farnum men. Timber as usual took what he wanted and their guns to trade in. He offered some to Bass but he declined.

"We can leave their bodies for the marshal here to tidy up."

As they stood talking the bartender sidled up to them.

"Marshals I heard about you and you did a good job here. I just heard from a customer that there is a man called Jose Rodriguez who is a Farnum gang member. Apparently he's over in Carthage visiting his sister, maybe you should go check him out."

"Thanks, yeah, I guess we should. Bass we need to get over to Carthage and find out about this Rodriguez."

"Carthage is about a two days ride from here Timber. We could stay here tonight first?"

Timber looked into Bass's expectant expression, "Yeah why not? Another soft bed sounds good to me."

"And a proper dinner."

Timber found no argument with that.

They found a suitable restaurant to eat in and talked over what had happened so far. They didn't see how it could have worked out any differently and they were both happy in going out to Carthage to see if they could rein in more members of the Farnum gang.

"You ever been to Carthage?" Bass asked.

"Can't say as I have." Timber answered.

"I've been there once, only know the place a little but I have an idea of what is where."

"That sounds good to me Bass, you can show me around."

"Sure thing."

They spent a night in the hotel then set out from town after breakfast the following morning. Bass knew the way or said he did so Timber let him work out the route. They rode on all day taking short rests when they or their horses needed them. They found creeks for water and grazing for the horses during the day while they ate biscuits and beef jerky. As the light began to fall they decided to find a suitable campsite which cropped up fairly quickly. It was close to a creek where some willow trees grew alongside it. A few rocks poked out from the grass and altogether it was a perfect place for them to stay the night. Bass got busy building a fire while Timber saw to the horses.

Before they had left town they had stocked up on supplies for the trip so they now got some of it out of their saddle bags to make supper for themselves. They ate well and had a pot of coffee heated to have more than enough cups of it. As they finished Bass seemed a little agitated.

"Something on your mind Bass?" Timber asked.

"It's maybe nothing but..."

"But what?" Timber came alert. It wasn't like the man to say that without a reason.

"It's just, you know, while we were riding I had this feeling that we were being followed."

"I get that a lot, often nothing there."

"Maybe but I got me a feeling," Bass shuddered and stared at Timber.

Timber stared back at the man who was fast becoming a friend, "You want me to check it out?"

"I guess we could both go look."

"No. One of us needs to stay here to make it look as though we both are I'll go."

"Okay, if you're sure?"

"Yeah, I'm sure. Just keep your eyes and ears open while I'm gone."

Bass nodded as he reached for his rifle.

Timber slipped out of the camp between the trees to get clear of the camp without anyone from outside seeing him. He then crawled some distance to get well away then crouching low he set off back the way they had come. He hadn't gone far when something alerted him over to his left. He stopped and slowly swiveled his head around to see what it was. Something or someone was out there close by. Timber drew a gun but didn't cock it as the sound would travel. He kept a hold of it as he advanced towards the shape he had seen.

He walked on conscious of making small sounds he hoped wouldn't be noticed. Then as he got closer he could tell it was a figure but it didn't look big enough to be a man. He carried on then suddenly he could see through the bushes he was up against into a clear area behind them. Then he stepped out holstering his gun.

"Tad Worthington, what are you doing out here?"

Tad turned around quickly to see who had spoken. On seeing Timber he relaxed but looked sheepishly at him.

"Timber, I er, that is I..."

"You've been following us, why?"

Tad stood back and let his arms drop to his sides, "The thing is Timber that as you know I work for the newspaper in Jacksonville and I reckon that the work you are doing in straightening out the Farnum gang will be a real big scoop for me if I can just witness it and write it all down."

"That may be Tad but what Bass and me are doing is very dangerous and will be for you if you keep on following us," Timber held a hand up, "Or try to join up with us. So the best thing for you is to just turn around and go on home."

Tad's face dropped as he heard the words, "But Timber I need a break and this could give me one."

"It could also get you killed."

Tad stopped talking and just looked back at Timber.

Timber looked back at him then said, "Get your things, you can come and stay with us tonight for safety but you go home in the morning."

Tad didn't need telling twice, he got busy and was soon walking back to the camp alongside Timber leading his horse.

Bass saw them coming and he waited for them to walk up to him, "Well now, looks like we have a spy."

"I ain't spying on you Mister Reeves honest, I'm just trying to get me a story."

"I done told him he can't stay Bass but he'll be safer here with us tonight." Timber said.

"Ah, can't I stay with you two," Tad looked anxiously for one man to the other. "I won't get in your way, promise. I just need this."

Bass looked at Timber and gave a slight nod of his head. Timber sighed, "Okay Tad but you do what we tell you, when we tell you."

"Sure thing Mister Timber, you can count on me."

Timber grunted and got himself a cup of coffee. Bass settled Tad down and gave him food and coffee for which he was grateful.

They all rode on together through the next day and arrived in Carthage in the late afternoon. They were anxious then to find any information on Jose Rodriguez and his whereabouts. Timber was figuring on checking out the sheriff's office in case he knew of the man but before they did that they called in at a saloon for refreshments from the trail ride.

They bought beer from the bar and Bass asked the bartender if he knew of Rodriguez. The bartender didn't have any information but as they talked a man standing close to them leaned over.

"Gentlemen, I know of Jose Rodriguez."

They all turned to see a tall well-dressed man smoking a cigar with a glass of whiskey beside him on the bar.

"Duke Duquesne," the man said expectantly.

"Bass Reeves, Jake Timber and Tad Worthington," Bass told him, nodding to each one.

"Good to meet you boys. Now this Jose Rodriguez you are asking about, nothin' serious I hope?"

Bass was about to speak when Timber spoke up.

"Naw, nothing serious we just need to speak to him on business."

Duke nodded his head then smiled at them, "Well he should be here tonight. We are having our weekly poker night, which is invite only," he added. "He fancies himself as a nifty poker player and he always joins the game when he is in town."

"How does a man get an invite?" Timber asked him.

Duke took a long look at him before he answered, "Oh I reckon I can arrange that for you, is it just you?" He asked looking at the other two.

Again Bass opened his mouth to speak only to be interrupted by Timber.

"Just me yeah. These other two have work to do," He gave Bass a wink unseen by Duke.

"Watch out for Jose, he cheats when he can, Duke said, "I let him win small pots last time but towards the end of the night, I set up a big pot and the overconfident Mexican went all in so I cleaned him out. Jose got mad but he was afraid to call me out. I have a reputation for being gun savvy."

"I'll bear that in mind," Timber said.

"Okay, glad to have you tonight, Timber. It ought to prove real interesting."

Timber agreed that it should.

"Y'all new in town," Duke said eyeing them all, "If you want someplace good to eat I can recommend a café in Mex town where Jose's sister lives called Mama Conchita's for good food." Duke was then called away so they carried on drinking.

"What you thinking Timber?" Bass asked grinning at him.

"I reckon this game tonight will be interesting. Stand by someplace close in case I need you. Better to have you there as back up."

Bass agreed with that. They finished their drinks and walked out. Tad was excited.

"I need to go find the local newspaper office and check in. I'll look for you later at the cafe." He strode off leaving the two marshals standing together outside the saloon.

14

"I THINK the time to get Jose is after the poker game tonight," said Timber.

Bass agreed not that it would've made much difference if he hadn't. Timber had that hard sound in his voice that Bass had come to recognize that meant he'd made his mind up and wasn't in any mood to argue the matter. Besides it kind of made sense. The game would definitely attract the man and if they let it play out he'd be lulled into a false sense of security.

"Okay," Bass said. "But could we get something to eat before we get caught up in gamblin'?"

"Not a bad idea," said Timber. "Didn't Duke say something about this place in Mex Town called Mama Conchita's? You like Mexican food, Bass?"

"There's some I like 'n some I don't," Bass replied. "But I'm willin' to give this place a try."

"Well, let's mosey on over there and see what's good."

Tad returned from his errand just before they departed and asked if he could come along. Timber hesitated at first, and then agreed so the three of them set off.

Mex Town was relatively easy to find. An area of town that was mostly adobe buildings of one or two stories with a white stone structure or two here and there, most of the occupants spoke Spanish instead of English, and most of the signs were in Spanish, with a few crudely hand-lettered signs in establishments that sought Anglo customers.

"Mama Conchita's' was a modest sized cantina located just inside the border of the district, and they'd been told by a man whom they stopped for directions when they got turned around at the start that it was owned by Rodriguez's older sister Conchita, and that this is where he stayed when he was in town.

"What if he's there when we get there and he starts a ruckus?" asked Bass.

"Well, we'll have no choice but to take him out there," Timber said. "We'd just have to try and make sure no innocent bystander got hurt."

A whole lot easier said than done. Bullets don't much care who they hit. Bass said a silent prayer hoping the outlaw wouldn't be at home. Not only would such a situation endanger innocent people but it would play heck with their eating schedule.

Bass felt relieved when they pushed through the multi-colored bead curtain that served as a door and entered the place and saw no one resembling Rodriguez. The place was busy though with over a dozen customers scattered about eating. A man wearing a wide-brimmed sombrero sat on a stool in the back corner strumming a guitar, which could barely be heard over the hum of conversation. They found an empty table not far from the guitar player and sat.

A buxom Mexican woman with her jet-black hair done in a bun on the back of her head came to the table.

"*Buenas noches, señores,*" she said. "I am Maria, what can I get for you?"

"Bring us a bottle of your best tequila. If you're gonna eat Mexican food you should wash it down with tequila," Timber said.

The woman brought a large bottle filled with a clear, oily liquid and three glasses which she placed in the center of the table.

"If you are *muy hambriento* tonight señores," she said. "Our *especial* is tamales with *chili frijoles, queso,* and *cebollas.*"

"Okay," said Bass. "I know that chili frijoles is chili with beans but what're the other two things?"

"Oh *señor* that is, how you say, cheese and onions."

"Well now that sounds just fine," Bass said. "Bring it on."

The woman beamed a broad smile at him. "If you are still hungry after you eat, just let me know," she said. "No one leaves Mama Conchita's hungry."

Timber and Tad ordered the same. They watched the sway of Maria's hips as she went back to the kitchen. Then when she disappeared through another beaded curtain Timber poured tequila into the glasses and they toasted to the success of the evening's mission.

When she brought the food, Tad looked at the amount and blanched. "That's a lot of food," he said. "I'm not sure I can eat all this."

Bass smiled. "Don't worry, youngster. I'll eat whatever you can't." He then dug into his food.

Unmindful of Timber looking at him in awe, he attacked his food with gusto.

"How can you do that, Bass?" Timber asked. "I know that chili's gotta be hot as the dickens."

"It's nice 'n spicy the way I like it," Bass said. "Not as hot as Cajun food, which is pretty popular in Fort Smith, being not all that far from Louisiana.

He immediately went back to the business of eating. To everyone's surprise, Tad managed to finish most of his. The tequila was pushed aside, though, and the young man asked for beer to ease the burning in his mouth. Timber called Maria over and ordered three glasses of beer.

"Three glasses of *cerveza* coming up," she said. "But do not overdo it misters. Beer and tequila can be a *muy potente* mix."

Bass had only taken a sip of the tequila, so the beer had no effect on him. He only drank half the bottle nonetheless.

"That chili must be pretty good, Bass," said Timber. "The way you're eating it."

"Best chili I ever had," replied Bass. "I notice you ain't eatin' yours. You oughta try it."

"I reckon I don't have the stomach for spicy food the way I did when I was younger," Timber said. "I think I'll just fill up on these tortillas and butter. At least this way I won't be hungry when I play cards tonight.

15

TIMBER AND BASS arrived back at the saloon fifteen minutes before the game was due to start and they had Tad with them. Timber left them at the bar and went over to speak to Duke who was sitting at a table.

"Is everything set for the game?"

"Ready as I will ever be," Duquesne answered, "but we have a problem. Little Willie Farnum is gonna be with Jose Rodriguez and maybe one or two more lowlifes. Farnum's real name is Willie Bob. It makes him madder than hell if someone calls him Little Willie to his face. Not only that, he is a loose cannon and quicksilver fast on the draw."

Timber nodded. Things weren't going down quite as he had hoped for but having another Farnum brother there was sure going to make things interesting. Maybe he could take down both of them tonight?

"Okay well whoever I guess. I'll be back." Timber said then went back to the bar.

"Tad you get yourself someplace well out of the way and stay there till I call for you. Bass we got another Farnum man joining us, Willie Farnum."

"Oh okay so two Farnum men tonight."

"That's what I'm thinking. It means we will have to rethink our strategy."

They all ordered beer and Timber noticed that Duquesne was just drinking water.

"Okay Now listen up," Timber said to Bass and Tad who was still with them. "I have an idea of how to take out both Jose Rodriguez and Willie Farnum."

They listened as Timber spoke then Bass said, "You call that a plan. Sounds more like a death wish to m, but my ol' mama, bless her sainted heart use to say, I would die with my boots on. I just didn't figure it would be so soon."

Duke Duquesne sat at the poker table limbering up his fingers by shuffling and reshuffling a deck of cards waiting for tonight's players to show up. The players were him of course, Timber, Jose Rodriguez, Lazlo Horvat, the town banker and worst poker player of the lot and C.R. Grainger, an area rancher.

Timber was still standing at the bar sipping beer and waiting for the game to start. Bass and the young reporter were sitting at a corner table playing a dice game called high low.

At five minutes to eight Lazlo Horvat strode in like he owned the place. He was a second-generation Texan whose father fought in the Battle of San Jacinto to gain Texas her independence from Mexico, Horvat was a ruthless businessman. He owned the bank and half of Carthage. Nevertheless, the banker was a good loser. The enjoyment of playing the game was his reason for participating.

Jose Rodriguez showed up at eight on the dot. Willie Farnum followed him in as well as two tough-looking Mexicans.

Now they were nearly all there Timber walked across to the poker table and took his seat. While they waited for the rancher to show up, Duquesne introduced Timber to the other players.

"It's not like C.R. to be late," Duquesne then said.

As he spoke a cowboy entered the saloon and sauntered across to the table and told them his Boss, Mr. Grainger's horse fell on him and he can't make it.

"That's too bad go get yourself a beer at the bar, tell the bartender it's on me," Duquesne told him.

The man thanked him and walked off.

"It looks like we will have to play with one man short gentlemen," Duquesne said.

"Hey my friend Willie Farnum can sit in," Jose said.

Duquesne looked at the other players to see what they thought. Timber nodded and the banker said, "Why not?"

Duquesne agreed and the poker game began. The rules were simple. Five card draw poker was the only game allowed. Twenty-five dollars was the betting limit and only three raises per hand. The game would end at the stroke of midnight unless a hand was being played, in which case the hand would be finished then the game would be over. Duquesne asked Pauly, the bartender for a brand new deck of cards. When the bartender brought them over Duquesne passed the box around so each player could examine it for tampering. Once everyone was satisfied with the deck Duquesne had Pauly break the seal and the game began.

In the beginning the game got off to a slow start and pots were small while the players tried to figure out their opponents' styles. Timber wasn't a great poker player, but he was a good one. Besides playing he had watched hundreds of games during his years as a lawman. He observed Banker Horvat playing conservatively. Jose was a skilled player but a poor cheater. Timber noticed that every time the Mexican bandit tried to manipulate the cards. Willie Farnum played impatiently like he yearned for a faster game with bigger pots. Duke Duquesne played flawlessly. Timber knew Jose was cheating but he couldn't catch him. The professional gambler controlled the game and only he and Timber knew it.

For a while every player won their share of pots with no one coming out ahead or behind. Then Duquesne called for a ten minute break so everybody could do their business and stretch their legs. When he came back inside, Timber moseyed up to the bar and ordered a fresh beer.

Bass left his table and walked up beside Timber. He ordered two beers and whispered "How's it comin' along?"

"So far so good," says Timber in a low voice. "When we start back Duke's gonna ramp it up and separate the men from the boys."

"I sure hope this plan of yours works, Timber. I really would love to see the sun come up in the mornin'."

"You and me both, pardner. Well, it looks like we're about ready to start again. Be ready if this thing goes all to pieces." Timber strode back to the table pulled out his chair and dropped into it.

During the next thirty minutes Timber won every other pot. Some of the hands are pure luck, but most of the times he won from Duquesne's card manipulation. The banker didn't pay attention who won or not he was just having fun. Jose Rodriguez won enough hands where if he suspected there was cheating going on, he didn't show it. Willie Farnum continued to play recklessly and he wasn't happy with only winning an occasional hand.

Around eleven o'clock things began to get real serious. Timber has won nearly every pot. The banker still didn't care, but Willie was becoming more and more agitated.

Jose wasn't a happy man. He realized something was going down but he couldn't quite put his finger on it. Then something happened that caught everyone off guard.

16

"I WANT A NEW DECK," Timber said.

Duquesne stared at him with an odd expression on his face. "Mr. Timber," he said. "We've been playing with the same deck all night. I see no reason to change at this late hour."

Bass, like a fly on the wall was watching from the back of the room. Other than he was planning to go for Rodriguez, Timber hadn't told Bass exactly what his play will be so all he could do was wait, watch, and be wary.

"I said I want a new deck gambler." Timber's tone was as cold as a January morning. "Is that a problem?"

"Yeah," Willie chimed in. "Open up a new deck. My luck's plumb died with this one."

Duquesne turned to a young man who had been idly standing by. "Pauly, would you mind bringing us a fresh deck of cards?" He didn't look at all happy with the turn of events.

The young man brought a new deck which he placed next to Duquesne. The gambler pushed the deck towards Timber, and nodded for him to open them. Timber slit it open and took a look, then nodded and passed them back to Duquesne.

"Okay, deal," he said.

With a speed and dexterity that amazed Bass Duquesne riffled the deck then put them down for Willie to cut the deck. After that was done he rapidly dealt out the hands. Bass was behind Timber so he could watch all the others and the room at the same time. He saw that Timber had been dealt three queens, a deuce of hearts and an ace of spades. He wasn't much for gambling but it looked like the marshal had a fairly decent hand. Timber removed the ace and deuce from his hand, turned them upside down and tossed them toward the center of the table when it came to his turn, and Duquesne dealt him two more cards.

When he picked them up, Bass saw that he'd been dealt the fourth queen and a king of clubs. Four queens backed by a king was a good hand Bass thought. Surely Timber had the table beat.

Timber looked around the table, pausing briefly on each man.

"Gentlemen," he said. "This has been an interesting evening but it's getting late. This will be my last hand so I'd like to make a proposition. What say we forget the limit and on this hand bet what we think the hand's worth. What do y'all think?"

"Makes no difference to me," said Duquesne. "As the bank I come out ahead regardless."

Rodriquez looked at him through narrow slits.

"You must have a very good hand *amigo*," he said.

"Now, friend, if you wanna know that, you'll have to pay," said Timber.

"Well, I'm all for it," said Willie. "It's 'bout time we played some real poker. I'm more'n glad to relieve all of you of your money."

Rodriquez snorted. "Very well I also agree." He didn't look any happier than Duquesne had when Timber insisted on a new deck.

"Well it looks like we're all in agreement," said Duquesne. "No limits on this hand. Mr. Timber, I believe it's to you."

"I bet two hundred," Timber said.

"Call," said Horvat.

Rodriquez and Willie also called.

"I see your two hundred and raise you five hundred," said Duquesne.

Horvat, Rodriquez, and Willie looked at the banker with their mouths gaped open.

Timber looked around the table. To Bass he looked as calm as a man on a picnic. "Everybody here got a thousand dollars?" he asked. There was some hesitation but eventually everyone nodded. "Good, because, I see your five hundred and raise a thousand. This is where we separate the men from the boys. Put up or shut up gentlemen."

Rodriguez hesitated but finally pushed in enough to cover both raises. He had very little left of his original bank roll.

Willie laughed as he put his money into the center of the table.

"Y'all are makin' me a rich man," he said.

Duquesne put his money in the pile. "I call," he said. "Show us your cards Mr. Timber."

Timber pauses for a few seconds, and then tossed his cards onto the table, face up. "Four queens, king high," he said.

Willie snorted. "Damn! You beat me." He tossed his cards down in disgust.

A silent but glowering Rodriguez did the same and leaned back with his arms folded across his chest.

Duquesne smiled revealing a gold cap on one of his front teeth. "I hate to do this Mr. Timber . . . almost." He slowly laid his cards down one at a time face up. "Four aces," he said. "And the five hardly matters."

As Duquesne started to rake in the pot Timber stood and pulled his right hand gun from under his jacket. "Hold it right there," he said. "I discarded an ace of spades so there's no way in hell you drew one unless you had it up your sleeve. I thought you were a dang card cheat and this proves it. Dang it, Duke."

Bass could only stand with mouth agape at the turn of events. This was totally unexpected. From the looks of astonishment around the table it was just as shocking to the others present.

17

EVERYBODY JUST STAY calm and put your hands on the table where I can see 'em," said Timber. "I got no fight with anyone at this table except the lyin' card cheat on my right. Nod your head if you understand." He waved his Colt .44 around. The three other players at the table did as they were told.

"Duke Duquesne," said Willie. "I always knew you was a lowdown cheat."

"Hold your tongue Farnum," said Timber. "I'm takin' this piece of trash outside, and I'm gonna punch his ticket...for good."

"Now hold on a minute Timber," said Duquesne. "I thought we had a deal."

"Shut up and get out of your seat." Duquesne stood up. "Take your left hand and lift that .38 pea shooter from your shoulder holster. That's a good boy. Now lay it on the table and take one step back."

Duquesne stepped back. "Timber, if you will just let me explain."

Timber picked up the revolver and stuck it in his belt. "Say one more word, and I'll shoot you where you stand." Timber glanced around the table. "If any of you want to see the show come outside."

Looking green around the gills, Tad stood next to him. "Do you have an extra revolver, Mr. Reeves," he asked.

"Why you askin'?"

"I want to have something to protect myself in case anything goes wrong."

"You stay out of the way, boy. Do you understand me?" Bass said. When the Marshal walked away, Tad whispered to himself, "Marshal Reeves, I will show you I am not a boy."

About half the saloon followed Timber and his prisoner outside. Motioning everyone to stand back, Timber moved into the middle of the street where he stood with Duquesne in front of him.

"Anybody who wasn't involved in the poker game stay up on the sidewalk. Mr. Horvat, Mr. Rodriguez, and Mr. Farnum, y'all stand about fifteen feet away from me and this card shark. Get right in the middle of the street so you can see what I do to people who try to cheat me."

Willie and Rodriquez glanced at each other then moved into the street to get a good look at what was about to happen. The banker hesitated, but curiosity got the better of him and after straightening his coat he walked out next to the other two card players

"Mr. Rodriguez," said Timber in a casual tone, "I believe you brought two more of your *amigos* with you tonight. Since they were watching the game, they deserve to see up close what I'm about to do."

Rodriquez looked at his friends and nodded. Anxious to get in on the fun, they hurried out to stand next to him.

Still keeping his gun pointed at Duquesne Timber searched the crowd until he located Bass Reeves. Bass rubbed the back of his neck and stepped into the street. Unnoticed, Tad walked right behind him.

Timber stared down at the five men standing in the middle of the street opposite him. "Mr. Horvat," he said, "As one of Carthage's leading citizens I don't think it would be proper for you to watch an execution tonight. I think you'd better skedaddle on home."

A look of pure disappointment crossed Horvat's face but unwilling to leave he stood his ground.

Someone from the crowd yelled out. "Go on home, Horvat, and hide under your bed till this is over with." The onlookers heehawed. If looks could kill the expression on the banker's face would have destroyed everyone who laughed. He stood a few seconds more then turned and bolted down the street. The crowd guffawed again.

"Shoot him in his big ol' butt," hollered Willie.

Once more, the crowd laughed. They were having the time of their lives.

Timber raised his left hand for the crowd to settle down. "Mr. Farnum, I can see y'all just fine from the light of the street lamps. Can you see me?"

"Hell yes. Clear as day. Get on with it. Me and my friends still got a lot of drinkin' to do before daylight."

"Just makin' sure. Wouldn't want you to miss what's about to go down."

Timber motioned to Bass, who ambled over and stood next to Timber. Hesitating for a moment, Tad walked out to stand next to them. In plain sight. Timber pulled the Smith and Wesson .38 from his belt and handed it to Duquesne. "You done your part Duke. Ain't no need to risk your life out here tonight."

Duquesne slid the revolver into his shoulder holster. "Way I see it Timber I owe you a might and I don't like to be beholding to any man. Willie Farnum is mine."

The four men stood with a couple of feet between them. Timber glared at the four men standing fifteen feet away. "

Gentlemen, we have a situation here. Things are not quite what they seem. My name is Jake Timber, and I am a United States Marshal. Bass Reeves is my pardner and a deputy marshal. Our assignment is to kill every member of the Farnum brothers gang. Chance Farnum is dead as is Jimmy Littlejohn, Rodriquez and Willie Farnum, you two are next on my list. Y'all are free to start the ball."

Nothing happened. The street was so quiet you could hear a mouse poot on cotton.

The two Mexican toughs glanced at each other. They were brothers named Rodolpho and Esteban Macias. Small time bandits, they were in way over their heads. Esteban, the oldest of the two brothers was about to ask that since they were not members of the gang if they could leave.

Just as he opened his mouth to speak, Duke Duquesne said, "What is the matter? Are you afraid Little Willie?" As he said that Duquesne's hand was already speeding toward his shoulder holster. Little Willie was a split second slower than Duquesne and no man could outdraw a bullet already hurtling his way. The oncoming slug smacked into his left eye. Little Willie Farnum never knew what hit him.

When Duquesne hollered out 'Little Willie' Bass Reeves, his eyes on the two Mexicans cleared leather dropping to one knee, as he did so. Still trying to figure a way out the Macias brothers barely unholstered their guns as two slugs from Bass's .45 tore into each of their bodies.

Rodriquez beat Timber to the draw and fired twice before the marshal got off his first shot. The Mexican outlaw's first shot went wide but his second whizzed past Timber's left ear. Before Rodriguez could fire again Timber's first shot hit him in the middle of the chest. The next bullet hit him six inches to the left of the first one.

In a matter of seconds the gunfight was over. Duquesne and the two marshals ejected their spent cartridges, replacing them with fresh loads.

"Some of you folks go see if any of those downed men are still alive," said Timber.

"These two Mexicans on the end are still breathin'," said one man. "This other one's deader than yesterday's bean farts," said another. "And unless this white boy can see with one eye shot out well, he's a goner, too."

With the adrenalin subsiding Timber realized his left ear hurt like hell. "What in blazes?" He reached up and felt his ear. It stung like a son-of-a-gun when he touched it. When he pulled his fingers away from his ear they had blood on them. "I'll be dad-blamed. I nearly got my ear shot clean off and I didn't even notice it." Undoing his bandanna he wrapped it around his ear as best he could.

"Whoever knows where the doctor lives go wake him up," said Timber. "One of you get the undertaker out of bed and tell him he's got two bodies to take care of.

"Three," said Duquesne, in a soft voice.

"Three?" said Timber looking in the direction where the gambler's voice came from.

Tears streaming down his face Duquesne was on his knees cradling a man's head against his leg.

"Somebody catch a stray bullet?" asked Timber moving next to Duquesne. "Good Lord! It's Tad." The shocked Marshal knelt next to the young man's head. Tad's eyes were open but the light was fading fast. "How you doin' kid?" Timber asked.

"I'm not sure, Mr. Timber. Am I gonna die?" The young reporter who desperately wanted a scoop was speaking in a monotone.

"Naw, Tad, you'll live to write the most exciting story the Jacksonville Sentinel has ever published. Hang in there, young man. The doctor's on his way. He'll have you patched up good as new in no time. Why…"

Bass laid a hand on Timber's shoulder. "He's gone Timber. All he wanted to do was help." Both marshals looked at each other and bowed their heads.

18

BUTCH FARNUM SAT on the front porch of the small home shared with his wife enjoying his second cup of coffee. When he wasn't raising havoc in Texas, Butch lived a quiet peaceful life where he was a respected citizen in Nacogdoches, Louisiana. Mind relaxed the head of the Farnum Brothers gang knew he should be planning their next robbery but he couldn't bring himself to do it. Although he wasn't old by any measure the gang leader knew if he kept on breaking the law, sooner or later his number would come up. The last train robbery had almost brought about his demise. There was plenty of money stashed away for him and his wife, Mary, to live out their lives in comfort. Besides no one in town knew his real identity. Here, he was just plain old Butch Franks.

Letting his mind wander Butch failed to notice the man riding toward his home until the rider reached his front yard. Ollie Farnum, Butch's obese, addlepated, older brother dismounted and waddled toward him. "Butch, I need to talk to you. I got some bad news. Can I come up on the porch?"

"This better be damned important Ollie." Butch sipped his coffee. Every now and then his big, stupid brother would show up with news. Sometimes bad or sometimes good, but often, information that Butch already knew. He figured this time would be no different.

"Mary," he hollered. "We got company, of a sort. Would you bring Ollie a cup of coffee with five spoonfuls of sugar, please?" He turned to his brother who by now stood on the porch with his hat in his hand twisting it for all he was worth. "Okay, Roly-Poly, let me have that bad news." Butch smirked.

Before Ollie could speak Butch's wife showed up with the cup of coffee he ordered. "Here you go Ollie," she said. "Five spoons of sugar just the way you like it."

Mary felt sorry for Ollie Farnum. He couldn't help it if he got shorted in the thinking department. Her husband always picked on his big brother considering him a stupid, fat, burden, a cross he had to bear. Ollie *could* be a real nuisance, but deep down he had a heart of gold and loved Butch and the rest of his brothers unconditionally.

"May I get you something to eat, Ollie?" she asked.

"No thankee, Ms. Mary. I ain't got no appetite right now." The big man took a deep breath. "Butch, I can't hardly say what I got to cause it hurts so much to say it."

"Mary, go in the house," said Butch.

"Honey, I want to hear what Ollie has to say."

"I said, *go in the damn house.*"

Upset by her husband's tone of voice, the petite lady put her hands over her face and scurried inside.

"Ollie," said Butch, "if you don't spit out what you have to say, I'm gonna get up and kick your lard ass all the way to Texas."

"O-okay, Butch I'll, I'll tell you." Tears streamed down Ollie's round face as he tried to say his piece. "Chance is dead. Willie is too." Rolls of fat on the distraught man's body began to quiver as he cried out loud. "What are we gonna do, Butch? What are we gonna do?"

Butch stood up his hands trembling at the news. "Naw, naw, that can't be right. You must be mistaken."

In between sobs Ollie managed to say, "Rodriquez and Jimmy Littlejohn, they been killed too. Oh Lordy Butch, what are we gonna do."

Reaching out Butch grabbed the back of his chair to keep from falling. Regaining his balance he dropped into the chair. "Quit your blubberin' Ollie, and tell me what happened."

The fat man undid his bandana and wiped the grimy tears from his face. After doing that he calmed down a bit and took another deep breath. "Chance got killed in a gunfight over in Palestine."

"Ain't nobody gonna beat my brother, Chance, in a fair fight. How many did it take to kill him?"

"Only one Butch. A feller named, named uh, uh... Dad gum it what is that feller's name? Oh, oh, now I remember. It's Jake Timber."

"Jake Timber! Oh, God, of all the people for Chance to go up against. I hear there ain't a man more deadly in a gunfight than Timber." Butch leaned back in his chair and raised his head. "Dear God what did I do to deserve this pain. Two of my brothers are dead damn it." He looked at his brother. "How'd the rest get it?"

Wiping away tears again Ollie said, "Willie got killed in Carthage while he was visitin' Jose Rodriguez. Them and two friends of Jose's got into a gunfight with Timber, a feller named Duke Duquesne, and a colored feller named Bass Somthin' or other. Them friends of Jose's didn't get killed but they got shot up real bad."

Butch let go a mirthless chuckle, "I can't believe this." He sighed. "How did Littlejohn die?"

Gaining his composure, Ollie spoke more clearly, "That Timber feller rode up to the Littlejohn's house outside Longview like he was a friend of Jimmy's. When the boy came outside, Timber shot him dead, right there on his own front porch. Somebody hidin' in the bushes shot another one of the Littlejohn boys. Killed him, too." Ollie stopped to take a couple of breaths. "The next day the remainin' Littlejohn brothers rode into Carthage seekin' revenge for their dead kin. Well, the same thing happened to them. They was shot deader 'n hell." Ollie acted like he was having trouble breathing. "Butch, I can't hardly breath. You know how I get this time of year. Can I go inside and lay down?"

Butch's mind was still reeling from the news. "Huh, what'd you say? Go inside, uh, yeah, okay go on, I got to think."

19

TIMBER AND BASS made camp near the same spot they'd camped when they were on the way to Carthage and after a somber camp meal sat across the fire from each other cradling cups of coffee in their hands both with their own thoughts.

Bass eyed Timber warily. The events of recent days seemed to have taken a toll on him, especially the death of the young newspaperman, Tad Worthington.

"It's really too bad about Tad," Bass said. "He was a nice person."

"Yeah," Timber said. "The kid had gumption."

"We gave him a good send off at least." Bass took a sip of his coffee.

Timber nodded and blew on his.

"Too bad we didn't get to know more about him," he said. "We don't even know if he had any family that oughta be told."

"I reckon the folks in Carthage will know 'n tell whoever needs to be told," said Bass.

Timber looked at him. His expression was unreadable, which was nothing new. In the time Bass had known him Timber had smiled probably two times, had scowled more times than Bass could remember but mostly he just . . . looked with that completely unreadable expression.

"I know you're right, Bass," Timber said. "I just wish we coulda done more for the kid."

"We did what we could Timber. Now, we gotta concentrate on findin' the rest of this gang so I can go home. I expect Nellie 'n my young 'uns are goin' crazy wonderin' where I am 'n what I'm up to. Don't you wanna git this job done and go home?"

Timber got a faraway look in his eyes. "Yeah, reckon I do."

XXXXX

THEY WERE HEADING to their hotel to pack up and hit the trail when Timber stopped in the middle of the road and snapped his fingers.

"Dang it Bass," he said. "I just had an idea how we're gonna flush the rest of these hombres out and deal with 'em for good."

Bass had looked at him and cocked an eyebrow. "What're you gonna do, send 'em an invitation?"

Timber smiled. One of the few times Bass had seen him do so. "Yeah, that's exactly what I'm gonna do. We need to get to the telegraph office."

Bass followed him just about as confused as he could be. His question had been sarcastic, but Timber seemed to be serious. Bass reflected on what he thought of as Timber's wild idea.

At the telegraph office he learned what the plan was and thought that Timber had finally gone around the bend.

He wrote the following message on one of the telegram sheets:

To: Butch Farnum:

My name is Marshal Jake Timber. My partner is Deputy Marshal Bass Reeves. We are the ones who killed your brothers and most of your gang. We're tired of chasing you. We'll be in Longview for the next two weeks.

Meet us there, or we'll come looking for you and we won't rest until we've killed the rest of you sorry cowards or run you out of Texas.

He'd given the telegram to the clerk with a stack of banknotes and instructed him to send it to every town in East Texas that had a telegraph office.

As they walked out of the office, Bass looked at Timber in disbelief.

"You don't really think that's gonna work, do you?" he'd asked.

"Can you think of a better plan?"

Bass couldn't. He shrugged.

"So we ride up to Longview 'n wait?"

"That's the plan," Timber said, "Just wait here will you, I have another wire to send."

Bass figured it was to Timber's boss so he waited for him to come out again.

XXXXX

A DAY later they were almost in Longview. There'd been no response to Timber's telegram before they left Carthage, but that hadn't worried him. They took a break and heated a pot of coffee over a fire. There wasn't much to be said so they both sat sipping their hot drinks.

They would soon be in Longview where as far as he could figure out there was nothing for them to do be sit and wait like sitting ducks in a shooting gallery.

He wished that Timber would show at least a little concern but the marshal's countenance was as placid as a mountain pool. After they had drained their cups they carried on riding.

20

WADE MORGAN SAT outside his cabin in an old cane chair, playing fetch with his coonhound, General Jackson. The big rangy dog wasn't much good at treeing coons but he was great at fetching sticks. The gunfighter was a lot like his dog, big and rangy, not too fond of work but "hell on wheels" at robbing and killing. With General Jackson as his only companion Morgan liked living in his small cabin in the middle of the East Texas piney woods. The closest town Sulphur Springs, served as the place where he bought groceries and supplies. Never a man to drink hard liquor and only an occasional beer, Morgan's needs were simple. An educated man. he read every book he could get his hands on and kept a small library of favorites in his cabin. His father wanted him to be a Baptist preacher and young Wade had been well on his way until the day in 1863 when Union forces stormed through his hometown. Looting, raping and burning everything they couldn't carry away the soldiers destroyed Fairesville, Georgia in a matter of a few hours.

After a number of years of robbing, and stealing and killing, Wade had acquired and given away a large amount of money - most of which had gone to the three churches in Sulphur Springs. Although not a member of any organized religion, Morgan was a spiritual man who believed in God and Jesus Christ when it served his purpose. He was drawing back the stick to throw it when General Jackson started barking like a maniac. Standing, he loosened the gun sitting in a holster on his left hip. He heard the horse before he saw it. Once the rider drew into sight, Morgan relaxed and strode to meet him. He waved. "What brings you way out here, Tommy? I know it's not a social call. You got something for me?"

"Yes, sir, Mr. Wade. I brung yuh a telegram."

"Light and get you a dipper of cool well water while I read the message."

"'Preciate it, Mr. Wade, but I got me lots of work to do back in town. Mr. Wilson, the telegraph man, said I was to wait and see iff'n you had a answer for me to take on back."

Morgan read the message, "I do have an answer, Tommy. Tell Jim Wilson to answer, I will be there. Can you remember that or do you need me to write it down."

"'I wull be thar'. I belive I can 'member thut. 'I wull be thar'. Yessir, I got it. Tell the missus Tommy Duran said hi. See ya Mr. Wade." Tommy kneed his chestnut mare and took off for town.

"I don't know how many times I have told that boy I am not married, but he just keeps forgetting. Oh well, come here General Jackson. We got to pack my war bag because I am back in business."

XXXXX

BUTCH AND OLLIE FARNUM left Nacogdoches on a Monday morning headed for the gangs usual meeting place in East Texas. It was three and a half days later before they arrived. The others were already there. When the brothers rode up, unchallenged, Butch's face was red as a rooster's comb and his mouth was set in a hard line. Before he dismounted the gang leader said, "How come none of you square heads challenged us as we rode up?"

"Lord knows y'all made enough noise comin' in," said Wade Morgan, squatting by the fire. "Boss, there's only one way into this box Canyon and Erastus is standin' behind a rock with his Winchester Yellow Boy aimed at the trail. If y'all had been strangers or the law he would've shot one of you. The sound of rifle fire would've alerted us in here and we would all have scurried to our prearranged hidey-holes. Now, if that answer is satisfactory this Arbuckle's fresh and begging for somebody to drink it. Y'all get on down and sit a spell." Morgan grinned and reached for two tin cups.

Butch dismounted and handed his reins to Ollie. The oldest brother knew it was his job to take their horses to where the other mounts were kept in a makeshift corral. The portly man had to remove all the gear from the animals, brush them and put them in with the rest

of the horses where there was plenty hay and water. When he finished that chore Butch would allow him to get some coffee.

Ollie hated his overbearing brother, but he knew he wasn't very smart and left alone he wouldn't survive so he did what he was told and waited for the day when he might get the upper hand and then he would show Butch Farnum who the real boss was. His chores

done Fat Ollie shuffled to the fire. When he got there he noticed four new men had shown up. Two of them he knew, cousins Verlin and Tunny Buckhalter. The other two were strangers.

Ollie slowed down. He liked the Buckhalter brothers because they were never mean to him. He stopped walking and took off his floppy hat. He enjoyed the soft spring breeze blowing through his sparse hair. Next time he got paid he was going to throw that old hat in the river and buy a brand-new Stetson "Boss of the Plains". He could hardly wait. The big flabby man looked forward to that day. He would get drunk, find a pretty whore and celebrate. That would be a lot of fun only he wished Chance and Willie could be there. Maybe his brothers weren't really dead. Sometimes Butch played tricks on him.

Ollie hoped this was just a trick. "Doggone me," he said to himself, "I bet they're gonna show up any day now and say, 'surprise, we ain't really dead. We just wanted to play a trick on ol' Fat Ollie. 'Course, I got to act surprised and not show them I knowed they was alive all the time." Jamming his hat on his head, the simple man waddled into camp. By the time he got there Tunny Buckhalter was fixing supper. The smell of bacon frying caused Ollie to salivate like a dog in heat.

The Buckhalter brothers were decent men who owned a small ranch in Oklahoma Territory. Neither one was a killer but since cousin Butch was blood they always showed up when he sent word for them to come help him. An unusual thing about the Buckhalter brothers was both of them enjoyed cooking. Tunny, the youngest enjoyed cooking with a skillet and Dutch oven. Verlin, who was the best man Ollie had ever known liked to bake. Biscuits were his specialty but the big rancher enjoyed baking pies and cookies, too.

"I sure do like it when you Buckhalter's show up," said Ollie. "I always know you boys are gonna cook up some mighty tasty vittles."

Turning the bacon in the skillet, Tunny looked up at Ollie. "Always good to get a compliment, Ollie, boy." Tunny called everyone except his brother, boy.

The cooking finished everybody lined up for their supper of bacon, fried potatoes, stewed tomatoes and a couple air tights of peaches. Two coffee pots were needed to make sure every man had plenty of Arbuckle's. They were right in the middle of their meal when a rider arrived at the camp. It turned out to be Buster Loman. Loman was an untrustworthy, back shooting coward who rode with the gang when it benefitted him to do so. The short, slender man jumped down from his horse and headed straight to Butch.

The outlaw leader watched him approach. "Evenin' Buster," he said, "grab yourself a plate. You just about missed supper."

"Just before I left my place to ride out here, a boy from town brought me a telegram. You need to read it." He stuck out his hand. Butch took the message and read it. The more he read the more agitated he became until he stood and paced into the darkness. The men could see the fire glowing from the end of his quirly. When the light went out Butch walked back into camp.

"Bad news cousin Butch?" asked Verlin.

The outlaw leader scratched the side of his head. "Huh," he said, "I ain't sure." He read the telegram to his men.

Right away there was hollering and yelling. "What are we gonna do Butch?" asked Ollie.

"We're going to get them law dogs, ain't we?" said Buster.

"What if it's a trap?" said Jimbo Scroggins one of the men who rode in with the Buckhalter's.

"Everybody quiet down and let me think," said Butch. He picked up his cup and walked to the campfire. Dumping out the grounds in the bottom he poured himself a fresh cup of Arbuckle's.

"Butch, boy," said Tunny, "don't somebody need to replace Erastus so's he can eat?"

"Shoot fire," said the outlaw leader, "I plumb forgot about Big E. Ollie go take his place and stay there till somebody relieves you."

"Aw, Butch I just ate, and I was fixin' to lay down on my soogans and take me a nap. Pick somebody else. Maybe one of them new fellers that rode in with the Buckhalter's."

When Butch's mother died she made him promise to take care of his addlepated brother for as long as he lived. To this day he had dreaded that promise. Sometimes he wanted to take Ollie out into the woods and put out his candle. The whining was the worst. It got on Butch's nerves until he always did something he would later regret. This was about to be one of those times.

Butch Farnum took a deep breath. With his cup of coffee in his hand he strode over to his older brother.

Watching Butch walking towards him, Ollie afraid he was about to get hit started shaking. "Don't hit me, Butch. Please don't hit me. I'll go."

"Stand up Ollie," said Butch, his tone calm. The fat man stood holding his hands in front of his face. "Every time you say something I disagree with you always think I'm gonna hit you. Right?" Ollie nodded. "Put down your hands big brother, I'm not gonna hit you."

"Promise you're not gonna hit me, Butch?" Smiling the gang leader nodded. Slowly the scared man lowered his hands.

Without warning Butch threw the cup of scalding coffee in his brother's face.

"Aghhh!" screamed Ollie, throwing his hands up to his face. He started jumping around like a monkey on a stick and yelling bloody hell.

"Holy smokes!" said Tunny, grabbing the cool pan of water meant for rinsing the supper utensils. He threw the water in Ollie's face then, with his brother's assistance, helped the poor man lie down. Tunny went to the skillet full of cold bacon grease and scooped out a big handful. While Verlin held Ollie down, Tunny carefully applied the grease to the stricken man's blistered face.

"When you finish greasing that fat pig up, Tunny," said Butch, through gritted teeth. "y'all put him on a horse and send his lard ass to relieve Erastus."

"He's not in any shape to do that, Butch," said Tunny. "The poor bastard is in shock. Somebody else has to go."

Red Roberts, the other man who rode in with the Buckhalter's stood and hitched up his gun belt. "I ain't tired," he said. "I'll go." The red-headed man took off to saddle his horse.

After a few minutes, Ollie, while still simpering began to settle down.

"You two Buckhalter's take 'Tub of Guts' and his soogans over by the horses," said Butch. "I'll be damned if I listen to that blubberin' all night. When you get back from that and Erastus gets here, I'll tell y'all my plan."

21

AFTER HAVING a good breakfast at a cafe in Longview Timber and Bass rode on to the telegraph office which fortunately for them Bass knew where it was. Timber thought it would be a good idea to send more telegrams out to ensure the Farnum gang all received one. They all crowded into the office to see the operator tapping away in a side office while a man sat at a desk taking the orders for telegrams.

"You all looking to send a wire?" The man asked as he looked at each of them.

"No just the one between us," Timber told him.

"Okay what'll it be?" The man sat poised with a pen and pad.

Hearing the message he raised his eyebrows more than once then when it was all told he looked up at them.

"You sure you wanna send this out?" He started.

Timber took his marshal badge from a pocket and showed it him before popping it back in again. He put a finger to his lips and held out a silver dollar as he said, "Now you won't remember who sent this message."

The man took the dollar, "No sir, I never can remember who comes in here." He ripped the sheet of paper from the pad and passed it on to the operator as Timber gave him a dollar to pass to him as well.

With the wire sent they all left the office then Timber turned to Bass.

"I have a call to make, I'll meet you at the saloon we used last time." He didn't stop to wait for a reply as he hadn't got the time to explain, he just got up on Scout and rode off.

Now where the heck is he off to? Bass thought, then shrugged and set off for the saloon.

Timber rode out to the railroad station, left Scout outside and walked out onto the platform. He had an idea when the train he was expecting would roll in but he confirmed it with the station master. It turned out he had just a few minutes to wait.

"Yes sir," the station master told him, "The three-fifteen train to arrive from Palestine will be right here presently."

Before Timber had time to do anything the engine arrived pulling four cars belching smoke and steam out like some massive black creature. It came to a stop at the end of the platform making Timber step back out of the reach of steam to look for who was disembarking from the cars.

Timber then walked along the cars looking for one person. He got to the end of the cars without seeing him so Timber wondered if he had missed the train. Seeing that all the passengers had left the cars and were leaving the station Timber found a conductor and gave him a description of the man he was waiting for. The conductor rolled his eyes and pointed his thumb towards the back of the train.

Timber turned around confused and started to walk in that direction but then partway to the engine he recognized the man he was waiting for ambling towards him. He stopped to watch Noah, the bouncer from Lester's Dance Palace leading the largest horse he had ever seen.

"I'd said I'd come if you called Timber and here I am," Noah said as he stopped close to him.

"Glad you have Noah, now who is this?" He asked going up to the horse.

"This is an eighteen-hundred-pound Percheron gelding named Brutus, and he's all mine."

Timber nodded as he examined the animal, "Sure looks like a good piece of horseflesh Noah."

"You bet your life he is," Noah patted the horse's neck.

"So what's going down Timber? I got your wire to come over here."

"That bother we had in Palestine Noah has got worse. There are more members of the Farnum gang than I thought and whatever help we can get will be appreciated."

"Okay, Timber you got it."

Timber walked out of the station with him and then together they rode down to the livery stable to leave their horses there then Timber took Noah off to the saloon where he figured Bass would be waiting.

Timber led Noah into the saloon to find Bass standing at the bar. Bass was surprised and beckoned them over.

"Noah, good to see you but what are you doing here?"

"I answered the message from Timber, I'm looking forward to helping you fellas out."

Noah smiled at him, "You're very welcome," he said as he gave Timber a nod.

Timber bought beers for all of them and they found a table where they could explain to Noah what their plan was.

22

It was an hour before dusk when Butch Farnum and his men reached a satisfactory place to camp just a few miles north of Longview. After the horses were taken care of and the campfire started the men sat around and waited for supper. Some of them smoked quirlys, some chewed tobacco, one dipped snuff and Butch smoked a particularly nasty-smelling cigar. With the help of his brother Tunny Buckhalter cooked their evening meal of pinto beans and sliced potatoes seasoned with onions and chili powder. Leftover biscuits, baked by Verlin for breakfast served as their bread for the night. As usual two pots of Arbuckle's boiled on flat rocks next to the fire.

After the heavy meal the men lay around in their soogans full and relaxed. Butch called Erastus Franks and Buster Loman aside to go over for one last time their missions.

"Buster, you go in first. I want you to spend most of your time hangin' around the saloon. Listen, listen, listen. If you hear something you think is important no matter how minor you may think it is ride back here right away and let me know. We are in no hurry. When I feel like we have enough information then we will strike the marshals down.

Erastus Franks had been a sergeant and had ridden with Colonel Butch Farnum during the Civil War. To the present day, Farnum still referred to him by that title. "Sarge, you are my biggest and strongest man. Your sole purpose will be to get rid of Bass Reeves. He's probably mean and real gun savvy. I don't care how you take him out, just do it. I gave you his description last night. That big bastard ought to be easy to pick out. Either of you have any questions? No. Good. Now go get some shut eye and you can leave in the mornin' after breakfast."

The three men settled into their soogans. Butch lighted another sour-smelling cigar, lay back and blew smoke rings. *Chance, Willie Bob, I swear on our mother's grave your deaths will be revenged. Once we kill those marshals we will ransack the town just for the hell of it and to teach people the Farnum Brothers' gang is not to be messed with. Who knows, we might even burn Longview Texas to the ground.*

23

THE BIG CLOCK in the tower of Longview's city hall building was just chiming nine when Buster Loman rode into town. It was too early in this part of East Texas, or any other part for that matter, for drinking alcohol but he was more comfortable in a saloon when in a strange town so he found one went in and ordered a cup of Arbuckles coffee.

"And it better be Arbuckles," he told the bartender. "Not that muddy water I hear ya foist off on unwary strangers. Oh, 'n make sure it's got a bit of chicory in it."

He smiled when the bartender's face turned pale. Loman wasn't a big or imposing man. Just five feet and a hair tall and weighing about one-twenty with his boots on he was no fighter. Truth be told the very idea of facing off against another armed man gave him an empty feeling in the pit of his stomach. To put it mildly, he was scared spitless of the prospect. Bartenders, though were seldom armed and probably just as scared of a fight as he was so he used bravado to put them off. He wore a .31 caliber Colt 'Baby Dragon' percussion pocket revolver in a tooled leather holster high on his left hip but forward for a fast cross draw when or if his bluster didn't work. So far he hadn't had to draw the thing and he was immensely relieved at that.

What he wasn't afraid of though, was dynamite. He was a master in the use of the stuff to blow things up and had been since he was twelve and had been introduced to it by an old miner who lived near the farm he grew up on. He found out early that he liked blowing things up, and that was why Butch Farnum had accepted him into his gang in the first place. A man who was good at blowing things up was an asset to a gang of robbers.

He'd been sitting quietly drinking his coffee, the only customer in the place when a short, stocky man with a silver star on the left of his brown vest walked in and went directly to the bar.

"Slow day Lester," the newcomer said.

"It is Deputy Barnes," said the bartender. "That fella in the corner yonder is my first 'n only customer today."

"Haven't seen him here before," the deputy said. "You seen him before?"

The bartender shook his head. "Can't say I have, deputy but little fella like that can't do much harm."

The deputy snorted. "Billy the Kid's a little runt but I hear he's killed twenty men."

The bartender's eyebrows did a little dance. "Lordy mercy," he said.

The deputy walked to Loman's table.

"Howdy," he said. "New in town ain't ya?"

"My first time in Longview, sheriff," Loman said. "Nice little town ya got here. Any jobs available? I'll do just about anything."

"First off, I ain't sheriff. I'm a deputy. My name's Rufus Barnes," Barnes said forcefully. Secondly, we do have a quiet little town and we intend to keep it that way. Not too long back Jimmy Littlejohn and some other members of the Farnum gang, three Farnum brothers, got killed not far from here by U.S. marshals. We don't want that kinda trouble here in Longview."

"My goodness," Loman said. "Four outlaws? How many marshals did it take to do that? Musta been a bunch. I heard stories 'bout the Farnum gang, and they're s'posed to be one tough group of men."

Barnes smiled. "Not a bunch," he said. "Just two. A marshal name of Jake Timber and a colored deputy named Bass Reeves. There's rumors that the rest of the gang's comin' to town to get revenge might be a dozen of 'em, I hear."

"Reckon them marshals are worried 'bout that," Loman asked as he looked up at Barnes for his answer.

"Worried? Them two? I don't think so," Barnes said. "Way I hear it; they're lookin' forward to the gang arrivin' so they can do to them what they did to the others."

"I sure don't wanna be around when that happens," Loman said. "Any idea when this gang is s'posed to arrive?"

"Nope, not a clue." Barnes adjusted his gun belt. "I've spent enough time jawin'. Better be on my way. Welcome to town friend 'n good luck finding a job."

When the deputy was out of sight Loman gulped down the last of his coffee stood and headed for the door. He had to find Butch pronto and tell him what was going on.

XXXXX

ERASTUS FRANKS WAS RIDING into town just as Buster Loman was hightailing it out of town in search of Butch Farnum.

"Wonder where that runt's goin'," he said to his bay, Joker. "Well, reckon we'll find out sooner or later. Right now, we gotta find this Deputy Reeves 'n take care of him. Hope I can git it done afore supper. I'd sure hate to miss the Buckhalter boy's cookin'."

He rode to the saloon dismounted, and went inside. Approaching the bar he said. "Y'all serve my kind in here?" He'd had the misfortune a time or two to enter places that hadn't heard that the war was long over and slaves had been treed.

The bartender looked at him with an expression of complete disinterest.

"Ya got money?"

"Indeed I do."

"Then yer the kind we serve here. What'll ya have?"

"Is it too early for a beer?"

"Mister, this is a saloon 'n it's open, that means it's time for whatever we got."

"Good, then gimme a beer."

The barkeep filled a glass, wiped the excess foam off with a piece of wood and set it in front of Franks. "That'll be a nickel."

Franks put a nickel on the bar picked the glass up and drained half of its contents in a few gulps.

"Is it to your likin'?" the bartender asked.

"It sure is." He put six bits on the bar. "Keep 'em comin' 'till that's gone. Say, ya wouldn't happen to know a big fella, looks a bit like me? Name of Bass Reeves. He ever come in here?"

"He ain't a regular customer, but I seen him 'n Marshal Timber come in here once a day for the last few days."

"Ya think he might be comin' in today?"

"He might. Ya can never tell. Ya a friend of his?"

Franks smiled. "Yeah, ya could say that. I'll jest take my time enjoyin' my beer 'n hope he drops by."

24

TIMBER AND BASS were seated at a corner table in a café not far from the saloon when Deputy Barnes walked in looking rather pleased with himself. In fact, Timber thought, he looked like the cat that just swallowed the canary.

"Hey marshals, have I got news for you," Barnes said as he approached their table.

"We sure hope so Barnes," Timber answered.

Barnes seemed to ignore the implied sarcasm as he sat down at the table." I seen me that Buster Loman character you asked me to keep an eye out for."

That made Timber and Bass sit up and take notice.

"Come on then deputy, tell us," Bass said.

"Okay well, I was doing my rounds and happened to go into Rusty's saloon..."

"How do you know the man you saw was Buster Loman?" Timber interrupted.

Rusty stopped and looked at him, "Why from the description of course. Man he's a weedy lookin' little fella."

"What description Barnes? Timber persevered.

Barnes stopped again and gave Timber a look, "You said to watch out for any strangers in town and that man sure is a stranger. What's more he was very interested when I told him about you two and what was going down and then," he put a hand up to stop any further interruptions, "when I left the saloon the little squirt came a running out of the saloon and skedaddled off out of town as fast as a jack rabbit with a coyote on its tail."

"Sounds like it must be him, Timber," Bass said.

"I'd say so, Timber," Barnes said, "you did tell me what to say if I encountered any strangers."

"Yeah I did at that."

"He sure reacted when I told him the story about the Farnum gang, just like you figured he would."

"Which way did that son of a bitch go?"

"He headed north."

"Okay, thanks Barnes, you did good. I'd better get out after him, maybe, just maybe he'll lead me to the Farnum gang." Timber stood up as he spoke.

"You going alone Timber?" Bass asked about to get up.

"I think that's best yeah. You ought to stay here and look out for any more strangers."

"Bass nodded, "Makes sense to me."

"Barnes, while Timber's gone keep a look out for Noah, tell him I'll be in Rusty's saloon," Bass said.

"It'll help if you tell me what he looks like," Barnes grinned at him.

Timber hurried out of the café just as Bass was beginning to talk.

XXXXX

BARNES LOOKED UNSETTLED at Timber's abrupt departure but Bass was beginning to get used to the marshal's way of doing things.

Bass gave Barnes a quick description of Noah. "When you see

him," he said. "Tell him I'll be over at Rusty's saloon," he reminded him.

After Barnes left, Bass headed to the saloon.

When he walked in he saw Rusty the bartender standing behind the bar and a large, dark-skinned man seated by himself at a table in the corner. He walked up to the bar.

"Hey, Rusty," he said. "Anything interestin' happen since we were in here last time?"

The bartender inclined his head toward the man at the table. "Colored fella over there says he's a friend of yours."

Bass turned slowly and looked at the man. He'd never seen him before but there was something about him that set off alarm bells in his head. Then it hit him. Thanks to his ability to remember everything he'd been told. Timber had given him the rundown on every member of the Farnum Gang and he remembered him mentioning the one black member, a man named Erastus Franks. Timber's description of the man hadn't been too detailed but the man at the table looked a lot like that description. There was only one way he was going to be sure.

He walked across the floor and stopped not far from the table.

"The bartender tells me you're claimin' to be a friend of mine," said Bass. "Only I ain't never seen you before. You know what I think though? I think you're an outlaw who goes by the name of Erastus Franks 'n you're part of the Farnum Gang. Am I right?"

The man looked up from his beer and glowered at Bass. "I ain't sayin' I am, I ain't sayin' I ain't. Jest who might you be to be sayin' such a thing?"

"My name's Bass Reeves. I'm a deputy U.S. marshal. I been workin' with Marshal Jake Timber to round up the Farnum Gang. So far, we've killed four of 'em. Now if Marshal Timber was here, he'd just shoot you 'n be done with it. My orders are to take you to jail but that's gonna be up to you."

The man pushed his chair back and stood up.

Bass, standing six-two, was accustomed to looking down at most men. Franks though, was probably half an inch or an inch taller than him and looked like he might be carrying nearly two-hundred-twenty pounds of muscle.

"Well now Mister Deputy Marshal," Franks said, holding up a fist the size of a small ham. "I reckon ya gonna have to show me ya got what it takes to bring me in."

That was all the confirmation Bass needed. This was Franks. Now, of course there was the problem of subduing him. It was not his nature to shoot first. He'd never had a problem in the past with handling men even men close to his size, in a man-to-man face off. He'd never, though faced someone who was bigger. Nevertheless, it was his job, and he would do it.

"If you're gonna resist arrest," said Bass. "You don't leave me a whole lotta choice." He opened his jacket to let Franks see his Colt.

"So, you're gonna be a coward 'n shoot me, are ya?" Frank said. "Ya scared to take me on without that there gun?"

Bass was astounded. The man sounded serious. He actually *wanted* to fight. Bass closed his jacket.

As he did so, Franks moved much faster than Bass would've expected a man his size could move. He saw the man's right fist coming at his head in a blur of speed and managed to jerk it back just enough so that it was a glancing blow off his forehead. But that glancing blow hurt like the dickens and for a second his vision was blurred

The near miss threw Franks off balance. Bass shot out his left fist catching Franks on the point of his chin and snapping his head back

Such a blow would've knocked any other man out cold but it only seemed to agitate Franks. He shook his head and swung again this time a right hand from his waist that caught Bass in the chest. It felt like he'd been kicked by a mule and sent him skidding backwards three feet. As he gasped, pulling air into his burning lungs Franks started toward him.

"Hold it right there, friend," a voice behind Bass yelled.

Franks skidded to a stop. His eyes were narrow slits of hatred.

Bass looked around and saw the big bouncer Noah, with his revolver leveled at Franks.

"Who the hell are you?" Franks asked.

"I'm a friend of the deputy," Noah said. "Now why don't ya back off 'n do what he says 'fore I plug ya?"

"That's all right, Noah," Bass said, still gasping for air. "I got this".

Noah chuckled. "Yeah, it looked like ya had him whupped."

"Just a matter of time," said Bass. "Now let me handle it."

"Ya sure?"

Bass nodded. He could breathe again now "Yeah. I got it."

Just as he turned back to Franks, the big man's right hand darted into his jacket and he started pulling out a revolver

There was a loud bang and the front of Frank's face dissolved in a spray of blood, bone, and flesh. Bass's head whipped around and saw the bartender aiming a shotgun. Smoke was still pouring from both barrels

"Ow," the bartender said. "This thing's got one helluva kick when ya shoot both barrels at the same time."

A thud caused Bass to look around. He saw that Frank's almost headless body had fallen to the floor. Noah the bouncer was gaping down at it

"Gawd!" he said. "Ya near shot his whole head off."

"He was about to get the drop on the both of ya," the bartender said, massaging his right shoulder.

"Well," said Bass. "I reckon you done saved our lives. Now you wanna put that shotgun down real slow afore you accidentally hurt somebody."

The bartender smiled. "I told ya. I shot both barrels. It's empty."

"Guess we oughta get somebody to move that," Bass said, pointing to Franks body. "I woulda preferred to take him to jail, but the grave-yard will do just as well."

"How're ya feelin', Bass?" asked Noah. "He got in a good punch to your chest there."

"He's the toughest man I ever fought," said Bass. "But I think I coulda taken him." He sighed. "No though, we'll never know."

Noah nodded. "Maybe ya coulda, maybe not. But that's one less of the Farnum Gang to worry about."

25

NOT SUSPECTING he was being tracked Buster Loman left an easy trail to follow. He stayed on the main road for five miles. Reaching a point on the road where the outlaw camp was hidden a hundred yards off to the left in a large copse of live oak and loblolly pines Loman turned and headed for the site.

Timber took his time trailing the outlaw. When he came to the place where Loman turned west he stopped his big bay, Scout and stepped down from the saddle. Pretending to be tightening his cinch he mulled over in his mind what his next step would be. Leaving Scout in a small clump of trees he decided to go the rest of the way on foot.

The thickly forested area made staying out of sight easy for him. Removing his hat to create a lower profile he moved from tree to tree, keeping an eye out for disturbed pine needles that lay among the thousands covering the ground. After fifty or so yards he caught the faint aroma of coffee being brewed up ahead. Crouching down Timber stayed as low as he could as he crept toward the direction of the smell. Gratified he was on the right track because the coffee scent increased he lowered himself to the ground and flat on his belly he crawled until he heard voices. Not able to make out the words being spoken Timber inched his way forward until the general sound of the conversation became decipherable.

"As far as we know, we're up against three men, four if the town marshal joins in, but I doubt he will," said Butch Farnum. "He'll probably be glad when those lawdogs leave town. The only thing about that is they ain't leavin' the way he expects they will." He chuckled. "Fat Ass, pour me another cup of coffee and this time don't spill it."

Ollie Farnum couldn't stand to be alone in their base camp so even knowing Butch would probably be furious that he followed them he had hid the supplies under a pile of pine tree limbs and took off to find the gang. It didn't take him as long as he thought and he found them an hour-and-a-half before Buster rode in from town. At first his brother scolded him for leaving the supplies unguarded but simmered down when Ollie told him how he hid them. Butch decided he would find a use for his big brother during the gun down.

"I sure hope Sarge can take care of Bass Reeves," said Butch. "I've heard of that man and he is supposed to be a double handful in a fight but I have faith in ol' Sarge. I ain't never seen that big ol' rascal lose in a tussle. If somethin' happens and he don't make it back there's still eight of us. Eight against three or four is pretty good odds in my book." Butch sipped his coffee then lighted one of his nasty cigars. Coffee cup in one hand and a long, black cigar in the other the outlaw leader looked the epitome of a confident man but on the inside a different story played itself out.

I miss my brothers, but they're gone and they ain't comin' back. I'll be real glad when this is over and I can go back to my sweet Mary and our little home in Louisiana. After this, I'm done robbin' and killin'. When I get home I'll be plain ol' Butch Franklyn, respected citizen and business owner. Life will finally be worth livin'.

"Boss," said Wade Morgan, impatient for Butch to get on with telling them the plan, "you were telling us how we are going to do this tomorrow."

"Oh yeah, sorry, I got to relaxin' and for a moment and forgot where I was. Okay, there's eight of us. When we go in tomorrow mornin', we'll ride in one and two at a time. Verlin I want you and Tunny to go to the cafe. Take Jimbo with you. Wade, Buster, and Red go to the saloon. Don't none of you stay together. When I send Fat to town, that'll be the sign that the dance is about to start. Fat's gonna go into the saloon and start raisin' hell. He'll say he's the last of the Farnum Brothers and call out the dirty dogs who killed his brothers. When any of the Marshals show up shoot 'em on sight. When you boys in the cafe hear the gunfire head outside and shoot anybody carryin' a gun. Everybody understand?"

"I know what I'm gonna do," said Ollie, picking at the blisters he got from the scalding coffee. "What're you a gonna be doin' Butch?"

"I'll be at the edge of town watchin' to make sure those two Marshals don't make it out alive if by some odd chance they get by all y'all."

Figuring he had heard enough Timber edged back from the outlaw camp. Duplicating the way he got close to the camp. He worked his way back far enough to where he thought he was safe and trotted to his horse. Untying the reins from the tree, Timber talked to his friend, "Did you miss me, Scout. I sure missed you." The animal nosed the pocket of his owner's vest. "Aw, you old nag, you're too smart for me. Okay, here you go." Timber dug around in the pocket until he came up with a cube of sugar. The big gelding devoured the sweet treat, and Timber swung onto his back. He kneed Scout gently, who then eased into a ground-eating lope.

26

AFTER WHAT WAS LEFT of Franks had been carted off to the undertakers Bass and Noah went to the café to wait for Timber. They were just about finished with their coffee when Timber walked in. He joined them at the table.

"There's eight of them," he said in his usual blunt way. "And just the two of us."

"Three," said Noah.

"Okay, three," Timber said. "They think Erastus took care of you Bass, so we got that on our side. They're likely to split up as soon as they get here and look for us here and in the saloon."

"That's gonna complicate things," Bass said.

Timber shrugged. "Maybe, but it might be a way to whittle the odds a bit in our favor if we split up too."

"Whoa," Noah said. "How's the three of us splittin' up gonna make the odds better?"

Timber smiled. When Timber smiled, it made Bass nervous because it meant that he'd come up with another of his hare-brained schemes.

"I have a plan," Timber said. "Here's what we're gonna do. Bass, you take Noah's shotgun and hide yourself in the kitchen here. Me and Noah will go to the saloon where Noah will be working with Chester behind the bar . . . maybe you can be getting trained to be a bartender. Bass, your job is to see that the ones that come here stay here, even if it means you have to kill 'em all."

Bass looked at the big bouncer with a worried expression on his dark face. "You sure it's a good idea, puttin' yourself in the line of fire like that?"

Noah snorted. "Ya think bein' the bouncer at Lester's Dance parlor was an easy job? Ya know how many hombres done pulled knives on me at that place when I had to throw 'em out for bein' a mite too familiar with one of the dancers?"

"Besides," said Timber. "He'll have the bartender's shotgun and a few other pieces of iron behind the bar. I'll be the canary in the coal mine. Noah will just be there to put the fire out if it gets too hot."

Bass shrugged. He wasn't too comfortable with Timber's plan, but didn't have a better one of his own. "Okay, I reckon that's the best we can do."

Timber leaned in and peered closely at Bass's face. "Is that a bruise I see on your face, Bass? How'd you get that?"

"He got that from his run in with Erastus Franks," Noah told him with a grin.

"Aw, he just got in a lucky punch," Bass said.

"Two," said Noah. "Don't forget the one to the chest."

Bass scowled at him. "Yeah, but I staggered him with the one to his jaw. Don't forget that."

"That ya did deputy," said Noah. "Too bad he had to cheat 'n go for that gun of his."

Timber looked from Bass to Noah with a question in his eyes.

"The bartender shot him in the face with that double barrel he keeps under the bar," said Bass.

"So we'll never know if you coulda whupped him," said Timber.

"I could've," Bass said. "It was just a matter of time."

"Probably." Timber looked at Noah. "Noah, you're gonna be the fox in the hen house. I'll stir 'em up and when the shootin' starts you take out as many as you can." He smiled again. "Just try not to shoot me."

Noah nodded. "In that little place I could hit what I'm aimin' at with my eyes closed so don't worry marshal."

"Okay," said Timber nodding his head, "Just keep your eyes open."

27

AT A FEW MINUTES BEFORE NINE, Verlin and Tunny Buckhalter rode into Longview. Pulling their horses up in front of the cafe they stepped down, tied their mounts to the rail, and walked inside. Both ordered Arbuckle's and sat back to wait for the fireworks to start.

Nine-fifteen saw Wade Morgan ride into town and settle in at the saloon. The bartender was the biggest man he had ever seen, even bigger than Erastus Franks. The enormous bartender told Morgan he was training for the job. Even though it was still morning, the outlaw ordered a beer and a shot of Old Grandad. He gulped the whiskey and carried his beer to a table.

By eleven-thirty all the outlaws were in their places waiting for Ollie to start the ball. Having second thoughts about his job in the attack, the oldest Farnum brother feared that Butch was setting him up to be killed. He was afraid to go through with his mission and afraid not to. Riding towards Longview his weak mind tried to figure a way out of his predicament but no immediate solution crossed his mind. Coming up with nothing Ollie rode as slow as he could along the road to town.

Timber left the cafe and got out into the street to look for the outlaws coming in. There were people about and riders coming and going. He waited for a minute until he had seen properly who was out there before he moved off. He wandered down the street towards the sheriff's office thinking things through. It was unusual for him to have men working with him especially men such as he had now. He had never really trusted anyone he had worked with before but these two sure seemed trustworthy, indeed they had proved to be more than once. So far, things were working out according to plan, he hoped it would continue that way. The sun was burning down and it was hard to look in the direction the outlaws would come in due to it being in his eyes. He squinted to look as he turned around at the sound of horses. It wasn't them so he carried on and sat on a bench outside the sheriff's office.

He sat there in the shade pretending to be asleep as he waited. It was a few minutes before anything happened. Then he saw riders coming in. Timber's keen eye recognized every one of the bad men as they rode into town even though the sun was in his eyes. He didn't recognize them all by name or their faces but by the way they carried themselves. He was sure the men he wanted had arrived.

He watched as three of men rode over to the saloon while another three had pulled up at the cafe. Timber hoped Noah and Bass were ready.

Noah stood behind the bar next to Rusty, who polished away at the bar top and tried not to appear too nervous. The bartender was doing a poor job of it. Noah knelt and checked on the firearms he had accumulated and placed on a shelf under the bar. Rusty's ten gauge Greener lay within reach next to a Winchester carbine and a .44 Remington. The big man carried his Colt .45 stuck in the back of his trousers. He was ready as he would ever be.

After Timber and Noah left for the saloon Bass took the shotgun Noah had left him his Winchester, and his Colt .45 Army Model into the kitchen at the café. The cook, a heavyset man with medium brown skin and peppercorn hair that was more white than black, scowled at him.

"What ya doin' in my kitchen?" he asked. "And with all them guns to boot."

Bass put a finger to his lips. "Not so loud," he said. "We're gonna be havin' some company soon, 'n I'm here to prepare a proper welcome for 'em."

The cook's eyes narrowed to slits. "What ya talkin' 'bout, man?"

Bass pulled his jacket aside and showed the man his deputy marshal's badge. The cook's eyes went round as he stared at it.

"W-what's that ya wearin', fella. Ya let the sheriff or any of his deputies see ya wearin' that 'n ya'll be in a heap a trouble."

Bass laughed. "I don't think so, my friend. Ya see, this here badge is the badge of a deputy United States marshal. That's higher than your little old county sheriff by a country mile."

Now, the cook looked incredulous. "Ya tryin' to tell me that a colored man's higher'n the sheriff? Now I know ya done gone plumb crazy. This here's Texas, son, 'n East Texas at that. These white folks 'round here git word ya goin' 'round sayin' you're higher than the white sheriff, they likely to introduce you to a high limb on the nearest tree."

Bass could see that the man was nervous about his presence. He needed to calm him down before the outlaws arrived.

"Say, mister," he said. "You ever hear the name Bass Reeves? Surely in a town the size of Longview you've heard of him. Y'all ain't all that far from Arkansas down here."

The cook scrunched up his eyes and scratched his head. "Oh, wait a minute," he said. "Yeah, I heard stories 'bout these colored deputy marshals they done hired up there in Arkansas, but I thought them was jest stories they tell when they settin' around drinkin' moonshine."

"No, the stories are true, and *I'm* Bass Reeves," Bass said. "I got hired near a year ago." He took the badge off and handed it to the old man. "That's a real badge you're holdin' and it gives me the power to arrest any man that breaks the law, white or colored."

Now, the cook was completely befuddled. Bass could tell that he was wavering between believing what he said and taking him for a completely insane person.

"Ya done arrested any white men?"

"Yup, eight or ten," said Bass. "I was down from Fort Smith to Paris to testify against a couple of cattle rustlers I helped bring in, when they asked me to help this other marshal, a white man named Timber take care of a gang of outlaws that've been ridin' roughshod over folks 'round here.

"I done heard of this Timber fella too," the cook said. "He's s'posed to be a real bad ass. Ya workin' with him? Ya have anything to do with killin' them outlaws I heard got killed lately?"

"Yeah, I helped Timber do that. 'Course, when I go after outlaws by myself, well not exactly by myself. I sometimes have a posse man or two 'n a cook. Anyway, when I go after outlaws, I try to bring 'em in alive 'n if they deserve to be hung, well, Judge Parker, he's the man that hired me he'll send 'em to their date with the rope."

"Well, I'll be doggone, ever since I been a free man I been hopin' our people would rise up and do some great things but I didn't think it was ever gonna happen. You a real honest to goodness lawman?" Bass nodded. "Well, Mr. Deputy Marshal Bass Reeve, ya got the use of my kitchen for as long as ya want. What ya wan' me to do?"

"Just go 'bout your normal work but don't mention to anybody that I'm back here."

"Yes sir, for sure my lips is sealed. Say, ya wanna cup of Arbuckles?"

"That'd be nice."

"Comin' right up. And I do believe I jest might have a slice of pecan pie I made for supper last night. Jest ya make yourself comfortable coffee 'n pecan pie comin' right up."

From that point on Bass had the run of the kitchen. The cook, Isaac Pettiman he said his name was kept his word. He took food orders and went about his kitchen chores and except for the occasional smiling glance at Bass stayed out of his way.

Finally when the March sun had reached its zenith Fat Ollie Farnum rode into town. Eyeing the saloon he dismounted and tied his horse to the hitch rail. Taking a deep breath and shaking like an aspen leaf in the wind he walked inside the saloon. Trying to ignore the other outlaws sitting around the place he ambled up to the bar.

Noticing Noah his eyes grew wide with anxiety. "You're sure a big feller," he said. "I've got a riding pardner who was the biggest man I ever saw before today." Stalling, Ollie tried to screw up the nerve to do his part. He glanced at Wade Morgan, who frowned at him and moved his head as if to say, get on with it but the tubby man wasn't ready yet. "Maybe you know my friend," he said to Noah. "Name's Erastus Franks."

"Is he black?" asked Noah.

"Sure is, so you do know him?"

Not exactly. I heard he came in here a day or two ago. Seems like a United States Marshal, name of Bass Reeves, had a disagreement with him." Noah leaned down until his face was six inches away from Ollie's. "Reeves blowed your friend's head clean off with two ten gauge shotgun shells. They say it was an ugly sight, blood, bones and brains all over the bar. What a mess."

"Oh my Lord," screamed Ollie and he ran out of the saloon and almost fell trying to climb aboard his horse. Once he was on it he rode as fast as he could north out of town. On the way he passed his brother riding in.

"What in the devil!" said Butch as his brother passed him. "This ain't good. I'd better hurry up and see what's goin' on." He gigged his horse into a lope.

Wade Morgan had watched Ollie run out, "Why that fat chunk of horse flop, fancy running out like that. I reckon it's up to me to start this show." He stood up and yelled at the top of his lungs, "I've come here to kill two marshals." He pulled his gun and started waving it around. "Anybody know where I can find those dirty scum bags?"

Buster Loman and Red Roberts unsheathed their guns and held them down by their sides in anticipation. Unknown to the two outlaws, Noah had done the same and stood ready behind the bar. Rusty prostrated himself on the floor and covered his ears.

When Ollie had ran out of the saloon, Timber stood up and loosened his guns in their holsters. He knew that was his signal to go so he began walking towards the saloon slow and steady, his eyes darting around him the whole time. He got up to the saloon and peered in the windows before he got to the door. He couldn't see too well through them but it looked like everyone was in their places. He walked on to the door.

Just before Timber walked inside Noah, not seeing the two outlaws hiding their revolvers under the table raised his Colt .45 and said to Wade Morgan, "Holster that smoke pole feller or I will blow a hole out the back of your head."

Momentarily stunned, Morgan did as he was told. Billy Loman raised his gun to shoot the unsuspecting Noah when a bullet from Timber's .44 shattered the silence and Loman fell on the table causing it to topple to the floor. "

Roberts, drop your gun or join Loman in hell," yelled Timber.

Red Roberts dropped his gun and raised his hands.

Timber had snuck in while Noah was speaking and had killed Loman in time as well as getting the drop on Red.

"Hang onto this man will you Noah, I gotta check outside." Timber said.

Noah came out from around the bar training a gun on Red, "I'll be glad to Timber."

Timber moved off as soon as he was happy that Noah had his gun on the outlaw then he went out the saloon heading for the café.

Bass had been in the kitchen fifteen minutes when he heard the sound of people arriving in the café. He peered through the window through which the cook pushed completed orders and saw three men armed to the teeth take seats at a table in the corner. He couldn't see their faces clearly but the amount of iron they carried and the way they sat so they could watch the door he had no doubt that they were part of the Farnum Gang.

He did a last minute check of his weapons and decided that in the confines of the café the shotgun and his sidearm were preferable. If he used his rifle he'd hit whatever he aimed at but a rifle slug was likely to tear right through its intended target and hit an innocent bystander. Shotgun shells on the other hand would rip and tear but were unlikely to pass through and hurt an unintended target. The same could be said of his revolver to a point. He checked the load of both barrels. Satisfied that shells were in both barrels he propped the shotgun against the wall and settled down to wait. He didn't have to wait long.

The sound of shots was muffled to him in the kitchen but the reaction outside at the tables indicated that the men there had heard them clearly and knew where they were coming from.

The three of them rose and turned towards the exit.

Bass knew then what they were about.

He pushed through the door from the kitchen into the café dining area and aimed the shotgun at the back of the nearest man.

"Hold it right there, gentlemen," he said. "I got two barrels of double-ought buck aimed at you. I can pull both triggers 'n pull my .45 'n get the rest of you afore you can turn around so I want you to unbuckle your gun belts and drop 'em to the floor. Then turn around real slow like."

The three men had frozen in place at the first sound of Bass's voice. They complied with his instructions and then turned to face him. Bass recognized Verlin Buckhalter and his brother Tunny, small time crooks who hung out in Indian Territory.

"Well," Buckhalter said. "Howdy Bass."

"Verlin, Tunny. What're y'all doin' ridin' with the Farnum Gang," Bass said. "Last time I heard of the two of you, you was up in the Territory. Who's this with you?"

"This is a friend of ours, Jimbo Scroggins. Jimbo, this here fella is known well to me 'n Tunny. This is Bass Reeves. He's a deputy marshal 'n if he comes after ya yer buzzard bait."

"You didn't answer my question, Verlin. Y'all members of the Farnum Gang?"

Buckhalter shook his head. "Naw. I reckon we might be third or fourth cousins of the Farnum's. Butch sent us a telegram. Said he had a payin' job that would be easy money. It appears he lied to us."

"I'd say you got that right," Bass said. "Now, we're gonna sit back down 'n relax until we find out what's goin' on across the street at the saloon."

The three men turned back to the table. After they were seated,

Buckhalter said. "No problem with that Bass," he said. "I got no hankerin' to git on your bad side and if your friends in the saloon are as bad as you I don't think there's gonna be anybody to pay us the money they promised anyhow."

Bass nodded. He kept the shotgun trained on the three men as he knelt and scooped up their discarded holsters which he put on a table behind him. He then perched his backside on the edge of the table and waited for Timber.

Butch Farnum was upset and confused. It was apparent to him that his brother had chickened out and ran away leaving his men in trouble. When the shot went off in the saloon and his men in the café failed to come out he knew his plan had gone straight to hell. He swung his horse's head around and took off at a gallop to retrieve some supplies at their camp and head back to Louisiana. His outlaw days would soon be behind him and the Farnum Brothers gang would fade into history.

Stopping in front of the café Timber heard a horse galloping out of town towards the north. Realizing it was Butch Farnum, he hurried to the livery and saddled his horse. Fully rested up, Scout was ready to run. Knowing the location of the camp and figuring Butch would head there, Timber pointed the big horse towards the north and gave him his head.

Reaching the spot where Loman had left the main road the day before he was startled by a shot off to one side. "What's that all about, big feller?" He said to Scout. "Reckon we'd better take a look."

Timber edged the big horse towards the sound being careful not to expose Scout or himself as best as he could. Closer in Timber thought he heard crying. Dismounting he left Scout in the cover of trees ground reined knowing he'd come to him at a whistle. Pulling a gun he snuck closer to the sound. What he saw when he reached the campsite caused him to do a double-take. Butch Farnum was lying on his back with blood oozing from a wound on his chest. He was breathing, but his breath was coming out in ragged gasps. Ollie Farnum sat on the ground beside him holding a revolver.

At first the oldest Farnum brother didn't notice Timber he was too busy bawling his eyes out. When he went to wipe his eyes he noticed Timber and raised his gun. "Hold it right there, feller and don't you come any closer. I'm Ollie Farnum, and I just shot my brother. Now, I'm just waitin' for him to die."

"If you let me look at his wound maybe, I can help him." Timber took a couple of steps closer as he spoke.

"He don't need no help to die. He's doin' that all by hisself. I love Butch, but he's always picked on me. Sometimes he hurt me real bad and he's always callin' me mean names like Fat and big Tub of Guts. Called me a coward. Well I bet after this he won't say those bad things to me anymore. I done showed him I was brave." Ollie poked his brother with the barrel of his gun. "I think he's dead. Do you think he's dead, feller?"

Timber looked at Butch and sighed. "Yeah, Ollie, I think he's dead. Just you hand me the revolver, now?" He reached out his hand.

"Okay, but I gotta do one more thing, then I'll give it to you." Before Timber could react, Ollie Farnum stuck the gun in his mouth and blew his brains out.

Timber shook his head and picked up the gun then he walked over to Butch and made sure he was dead which he was. He took his gun and then searched both bodies. The only useful things he found was a few dollars. He then whistled for Scout and soon he was riding off back to town. He was keen to find out how Bass and Noah had got on.

28

TIMBER GOT into town and went to the saloon to check up on Noah. He had Bass there with him. Timber worked with them and Barnes to get all the outlaws still alive either to jail or on their way home. Timber then ordered beers for all of them and got them to sit around a table to talk.

"So let me get this straight," said Noah. "The men who came with Butch Farnum that were set free weren't regular members of the gang so you set them free and told them to leave Texas for good. Is that right Timber and, if so, why?"

"The Buckhalters and their two men were hired to do a job that put them in the wrong place at the wrong time," said Timber sipping his beer. "As long as they stay out of Texas they're safe. If they ever come back and I find out about it I will personally snuff out their candles. Morgan is another matter. He will either be hanged or spend the rest his life in prison."

"I work mostly in Indian Territory," said Bass sipping his beer as he always did not being much of a drinker. He felt the need now though to be sociable and a part of the group "I know where the Buckhalters stay. And I'll put the word out to the rest of the deputies up there to keep an eye on 'em. I don' think they'll step outta line, though."

Timber nodded, "That sounds good to me Bass."

"Gentlemen," said Noah as he stood up, "it's time I was getting back to the Dance Palace before my brother decides I am replaceable. It has been fun. Let's do this again sometime." He gave their hands a vigorous shake and strode from the saloon.

"Good man," said Timber watching him walk out.

"Yes sir he sure is," said Bass, finishing his beer. He stood and reached out his hand to Timber. The marshal rose from his chair and clasped the outstretched hand. "Timber, like the man said, we have to do this again sometime. It's time I got back to Nellie, she'll be wonderin' 'bout me." He tipped his hat and disappeared through the swinging doors.

Timber watched him go then called for another beer. While he waited, he dug into a pocket and pulled out a dogeared deck of cards. "Been awhile since I played solitaire," he said to himself. "Hope I remember how to play." He chuckled and began to shuffle the cards.

Made in the USA
Columbia, SC
18 November 2024